ACCADEMIA

Dear Frank,
just a brief scene
in the epic film
we lived!
with love,
Giotti

Dec. 29, 1997

Prose Series 38

Giose Rimanelli

ACCADEMIA

A Novel

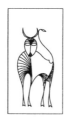

Guernica
Toronto/New York/Lancaster
1997

Antonio D'Alfonso, Editor
Guernica Editions Inc.
P.O. Box 117, Station P, Toronto (ON), Canada M5S 2S6
250 Sonwil Drive, Buffalo, N.Y. 14225-5516 U.S.A.
Gazelle, Falcon House, Queen Square, Lancaster LA1 1RN U.K.

Legal Deposit — Second Quarter
National Library of Canada
Library of Congress Catalog Card Number: 96-78720

Rimanelli, Giose, 1926-
Accademia
(Prose series ; 38)
ISBN 1-55071-015-X
I. Title. II. Series.
PQ4839.I53A73 1997 813'.54 C97-900071-8

Roses are planted where thorns grow.

John Donne

Non c'è rosa senza spine,
non c'è amore senza pene.

Italian Proverb

. . . any work, any novel tells, through the events of
its plot, the story of its own creation, that is, its own
story. The sense of a work consists in telling about
itself, in speaking to us of its own existence . . . The
very existence of a novel is the last link in the chain
of its plot: where the story that is narrated ends,
precisely where the story that narrates, the liter-
ary story begins . . .

Tzvetan Todorov,
Literature and Signification

O rose, thou art sick;
The invisible worm
That flies in the night,
In the howling storm,
Has found out thy bed
Of crimson joy,
And his dark secret love
Does thy life destroy.

William Blake

1

Summer had crammed with people the meadow and all the small structures surrounding the glass house. Now it is emptying out. Academic life, chaotic and monotonous, is starting all over again. It's already completely programmed. But the feeling remains motionless.

Meanwhile I record the passing days, the things of yesterday and today, to the point where memory makes me dizzy. The barometer is rising but the expectation is the journey.

The sun, lacking rays, is overly big. Fixing one's gaze on it is like no longer seeing. The aim is not to remember but to save what I do not know in the moment that I know what I am not saving.

I go out to the brick guest house in the woods beyond the meadow and see Dino still carrying his backpack. My son Dino returned to Italy on the twelfth bringing Revlon perfumes for his mother, a dozen of old Beatles records for his brother Sandro, and a new tennis racquet for himself. Then I go to the study across the meadow and see Daniel at the piano, practicing. My son Daniel has also just returned from a visit, to his grand mother in New Canaan, Connecticut. He brought back with him fifty dollars neatly folded in the pocket of a chick trendy suit, along with a minuscule iguana in a miniature Philip Johnson's *Glass House* that looks like a coffin, just as much as this house of mine, a cheap imitation of it in glass and steel and huge canvases inside representing fake moving walls.

Lisa had driven him back. Her fingernails and lips were chewed up, and she looked weary and rancorous.

Dino is less restrained than Daniel whom he disparagingly calls "the kid." He is two years older than Daniel and engages in all-round sports — swimming, cycling, soccer, fencing, and horse horsemanship — while Daniel is still a polliwog in a pool. Dino admittedly masturbates; he would like to have a woman but doesn't yet know how to go about it. He will be grabbed up soon, though, since he's good looking and knows it. His English isn't so good, but it doesn't bother him in the least; his communication with others takes the form of an explosive sensuality.

All this repels Daniel. This so-called brother is actually a stranger as was Sandro for that matter, whose acquaintance he had made only last summer. Nor has Daniel forgotten Sandro, his father's eldest son, a youngster savage and malign, a sly *provocateur,* who sported a scornful mustache in the manner of a West Point cadet. In Sandro's eyes Daniel "the kid" was a fat pinkish piglet to be roasted on a spit. Through him Lisa intuits Sibyl's revenge, Sibyl the Roman lady whose man had walked off on her wantonly and capriciously, subsequently dubbing divorce love.

One day Daniel fell in the canal on Cape Cod, his first real terror of his life. He was drowning in the water under the eyes of this guffawing stranger who watched him from the bridge. Even his father, the father of both of them, didn't as much as budge an inch. He remained seated under an enormous beach umbrella, absorbed in a book.

But there was really nothing to be done. The father indeed was the least concerned since he was the one really marginal to the situation. For the children, the offspring of two marriages and reared in two different countries, appeared to him only as intermittence of lights and shadows amid insane peals of laughter.

The only thing that still interested this old man, exiled from all affections, exiled from himself, exiled from the great causes that enjoin participation, was the wild journey into the soul of this Princess of his, fourteen years his junior, on which he drunkenly fed in a parody of incest. He was a child.

Although sex is the most unreal of fantasies, it gives one joy and repose. Sex is another life at the portals of death.

Our sex life, however, is poisoned by social monsters, boredom, porno-fantasy, and lukewarm blood. Lisa knows this, but she always demands more, and now. She is projected towards regions unknown, and all that is left for me is to await the new unknown. It will be a shattering event, but even that will pass. I hear the blow arriving from the rotten shrubs of our town, Anabasis, Nabokov County, Appalachia, U.S.A. It would be possible to make a souvenir photo of Anabasis, lightly over-exposed with a black and white 35mm film.

The reason of diaries: Things, happenings, recorded or remembered because we are separated from them. We have remained alone.

2

On the fourteenth the carpet cleaners came. On the fifteenth the refrigerator repairman showed up. And the sixteenth saw the arrival of Judy Madison from New Orleans.

She slept in the small glass room area, by us called Pearls Gate, or, in French, *Porte de Jade*. She refused to use the guest house, or the study, or the monkeys' lab which was, now, temporarily emptied of inhabitants.

She didn't feel like driving directly to her apartment on Cyrus Street, in the old part of town. And so I knew that she wanted me, or Lisa, in order to forget herself.

The two women find peace in each other's company. It is a friendship built on tremors, anxieties, and confidences that exclude the male and the element of struggle.

Judy is much more covetous and gloomy than Lisa. The lust in her eyes is always a prenatal journey promised to the crew. Judy is as dark and tender as an oriental night, while Lisa projects a liquid pomeridian lustfulness that sets romantics sighing.

Judy made some phone calls, one of which was to Punks, that is Andrew, the deserted husband. But then she abruptly hung up.

"You are separate entities now," I reminded her. "To what purpose?"

"I'd like to go there and burn his damn barn down with him inside it and all the shit he produces," she replied in a rattle-like voice.

"It didn't seem to bother you when you were with Punks," I pointed out with seeming indifference.

Because some of Punks' ideas are mine (which I made available to him) when Judy is disparaging Punks' shit it seems that she's also disparaging my "shit." But she never understood Andrew (astrologically a Cancer), nor has she read his only but seminal book.

Andrew is a laboratory chemist who experiments with guinea pigs. His diagnoses are very often wrong. Only years later did his notebooks reveal that he had arrived at an exact hypothesis which, however, was considered incorrect at that time. The technical means for verification and of the skepticism of his colleagues were the cause of his "downfall."

In his early young manhood he had published an annotated edition of Robert Chambers' book on evolution, *The Vestiges of the Natural History of Creation,* which had first appeared anonymously in 1844. Andrew commented on Chambers more as historian than as chemist. He also discussed the geologist Lyell whose ideas on species that had become extinct had influenced Darwin as much as he had been influenced by the Malthusian concept of power-population, a work published in 1798.

Andrew's thesis, though based on the history of science, tried ("creative analysis") to determine whether or not biology was indeed an exact science, and whether or not it conformed to the same principles that governed other sciences. The advances made by astronomy, physics, and chemistry had been amply recorded down the centuries. Biology, on the contrary, was a subject so recent and so vast that it was difficult, if not altogether impossible, to establish where and when it started; that is, where it began and ended at this particular point in time.

Since all thought depends on the brain, Andrew questions whether frontiers exist between philosophy and biology. And since all living things are made up of molecules, may it not be possible that the study of life derives its basic principles from those governing physics and chemistry?

These ideas, only seemingly hypothetical, ultimately led Andrew to the exploration of metaphysical problems. Hence it should occasion no surprise to note that his commentaries on the *Vestiges of Natural History* concluded with embarrassing questions: Was it absolutely proven that fixed laws existed in the universe? And if such laws did exist, how many of them were known by the human being?

Andrew was brilliant, clever, sensuous, and, ultimately, useless. Unfortunately, his exploration of existence was wholly directed towards the useless: For him, at least, it was a form of active boredom, the presupposition of which was a hedonistic, possibly painless, life style. The artist, as he often repeated, was an atemporal, asexual being constantly in a state of pregnancy. And this pregnancy defined the useless better than did any other expression.

In order to pay for the Bentley, the Morgan, and the Land Rover, crouched in his enormous garage, Andrew produced and directed short underground films in the New York tradition of Andy Warhol and Jonas Mekas, the costs of which were met by generous grants from a long list of educational foundations. One of these films, marked by the wit and melodrama that could pass as an experiment in iconography, also bore the signature of the sociobiologist Simon Dona, the "I" of this narrative.

Academically, I am a physical anthropologist, better known to cynics in American circles for the endless interpolations that my writings (based on experiments with monkeys of the Macaque species) may offer to the old adage: Woman's monogamous; man is polygamous.

One review assessed the many essays I wrote in the following unflattering way: "Simon Dona's studies lay great stress on the notion of two-animal man. There exists, namely, a feminine human nature and a masculine human nature, and these two natures exhibit an extraordinary difference between them, even though these differences, often and somehow, are masked by the compromises of heterosexual relations and by moral injunctions. It would follow, therefore, that a sexual "estrangement" exists between male and female. The dispositions and the sexual desires between male-female revolved themselves in the process of mutual adaptiveness. Dona went so far as to formulate the concept that if one of the sexes is good, the other is poison."

The film, titled *The Twelfth Macaque,* was in part derived from the sexual theories of Tiger-Fox, Morris, Dawkins, Maynard Smith which maintained that man can be divided into *one-animal* men and *two-animal* men. But the film was mainly based on my own personal convictions concerning the bonnet monkey, the monkey with the crop-tail and cap-like head and whose hair hangs like trinkets on his wily face, who swims to hunt sea-crabs and climbs coconut trees to steal coconuts.

It was nothing else but a short film made to amuse and provoke the eggheads (and their wives and lovers) at the University. Yet many still reproach us for it, especially the compact band of female colleagues.

Rafael Oviedo de Bernalbe generally spent his academic vacations at the Vatican Library in Rome, masquerading alternatively as a Basque revolutionary and as an agent of *Pro Deo*. He was gentle, bearded and sly, gliding through the corridors with a conspirational air. When he was all by himself in his novice's cell, he played the flute. Disappointed in married love, and disenchanted with women in general, he found for years a pondered pleasure in watching birds during copulation.

Although Fernán Caballero's book, *La Gaviota,* no way referred to homosexuality behavior among sea gulls, it led him to closely study the hymeneal behavior of seagulls. The study was further encouraged, according to him, by Virgil's assertion that "they can because they think they can." In fact, he spent a whole summer studying the sob-like noises of seagulls in the grottoes of the Tremiti archipelago facing the promontory of Gargano in Italy. He wanted to definitely establish whether or not their lamentations were due to the tragic death of the Greek hero Diomedes, as handed down to us by Pliny and Theophrastus.

De Bernalbe came back convinced that at least eighteen percent of seagulls were lesbian. In one of his reports to the "Feathers Gaviotanos," which in some way was linked to the American Association for the Advancement of Science, he demonstrated how certain female gulls assumed the male role, and how the birds finally formed a stable union more or less on the type existing between heterosexual seagulls. They went through the motion of copulation, depositing sterile eggs, and defending their nest like any other.

De Bernalbe found no evidence, however, of homosexuality among male seagulls. His error was blasphemous. Thus when he proposed that it would be *of interest* to give a seminar on the theme *The Role of*

Sea Gulls, the female colleagues reacted fiercely. Worst of all he had the proposal circulated anonymously.

At that time I was called upon to voice a point of view on the female seagull, and though reluctant, I declared that she was not "genetically focalized."

Immediately, my female colleagues looked at me with suspicion: Was I too discriminating against women in Academe?

No, of course. But that was a strange, Vietnamized, so to speak, epoch: The 1970s. Violence ran along a tightrope, and love was sparse and twisted, striking a precarious balance between morality and blasphemy. Often it was pure violence. And violence was as binding as love. There was much quarreling, and quarreling by no means precluded violence because it was already violence. The academics engaged in it with words knowing well that a word could be as destructive as the blow of a hand. Consequently violence, be it verbal or physical, invited vengeance.

Sex became a battleground in those years and pleasure a bone of contention. There was much talk of sado-masochism: Perversion was violently injected into pleasure to such an extreme degree that pleasure became obscure, cruel, criminal.

It was only later that we realized that everything we did out of love was no different from what we did out of hatred. Everybody talked; few listened.

The College was the mother to whom we attributed guilt and wonder, death and metaphor, hope and judgment, faith and malice, and sentimentalism to boot. The result was that today the reaction is harsh and uncompromising.

Now Judy, bereft of Andrew, was on the prowl for men and women, a perennial and frustrating anxiety of eternal repose (or gratification) that she called transcendental meditation, trying to attract Lisa's vague into the orbit of her shadow — with me between the two of them, observing and writing.

She ran a high fever at midnight, and asked me to take her temperature. At 2 AM she moved the canvas wall, came into the master bedroom area, and slipped into the bed. She had the chills and wanted me to keep her warm. Nobody talked. Our two bodies held each other in the darkness, pierced at intervals by sobs and nervous peals of laughter.

We were on a trip now. I was the horse, she the carriage. And we were alone and depleted, devoid of purposes or desires. But the jumping about between the squeaking of wheels and pieces of furniture, laments and neighing, was like rerunning the 200 miles that separated us from New Canaan where Lisa slept alone in the old bed that she slept in as a girl.

"Tomorrow," I said to Judy, "I'll phone Lisa and tell her that we have done something that we have always wanted to do."

"She'll answer that the three of us should have done it together."

Only now do I realize that violence thus employed no longer has any significance: It becomes part of the pleasure, our failure.

Awake, I watched her all night, feeling my vacuum.

3

On the following day Judy was in a demure state and wanted me to take her to the laboratory. The cockroaches in residence heard the key turning in the lock and passed along the news of her arrival among themselves. The darkness was suddenly pierced by the cone of light from Judy's infrared pocket lamp, revealing the oscilloscope, the cork ball, boxes of cereals, a dripping sink, moist plastic plates, still water in flower-pots, a half-rotten apple left in the open, a garbage can with a half-opened cover, dry crumbs of cat food in a yellow oval plate.

Abruptly the light focused on a pair of mahogany-colored insects on a white, wooden gangway. They were about five centimeters long and their antennae were locked in a duel.

"Professor Roe and Doctoress Schar are rubbing noses," Judy explained, and added: "They are sniffing each other with their antennae, and I'm certain that they know one another's identity."

"Do you name your cockroaches after people you know?" I asked.

"I've got about thirty-five of them here. And even if I don't recognize them perfectly, I call them Dr. Kenneth, Dr. Berta, Dr. Michael, Dr. Dale, Dr. Noam, Dr. Louis, Dr. Charlotte. In this Accademia they are my academicians."

"In Rome they call them *bacarozzi,* and they are not academics but religious, priests in general."

"Do you see that one over there? That's you."

I followed the cone of light as it fell on a nearby spur on which a huge male roach was bent over in an interdictive posture.

"It's almost certain that Dr. Dona will remain there for hours, probably all day and all night prohibiting access to his turf."

I laughed nervously. This lady entomologist was more fragile than I thought. Keeping one eye on the door, I interjected:

"Actually I don't sufficiently protect my turf, my grass meadow, my glass house. My bed is a three-quarter size. You've climbed into it. Now what will you do?"

"I'm taking the train."

I laughed recalling that Judy Madison was at that time an assistant to Matthias Freedman, professor of comparative neuroendocrinology. For decades his passion had been the study of cockroaches, "since they are tough tiny creatures that survive every kind of experimental humiliation." Freedman's parents, who had been destroyed in Dachau's 'experimental' ovens, had observed in a letter to an American cousin, Ethel, that the life of cockroaches was better than that of prisoners in the hands of the Nazis. Ethel and the very young Matthias sat for months in the witness box at the Nuremberg trials which dragged on from 1945 to 1946 in order to bring the Nazi ringleaders to judgment. Matthias' eyes focused in astonishment on those big time murderers: And in a flash he understood that the study of cockroaches is the study of survival. His books on the cellular nerves and the behavior of insects are famous; one of them is a combat manual that is often found in the library of American family.

Judy Madison's studies, in syntony with Freedman's, concerned the six-footed residents of the university laboratory, numbered with adhesive tape whose movements were followed and observed on different nights of the week and then registered on a magnetic tape. Judy's interests were limited to the natural behavior of the cockroaches, to their way of communicating, eating, fighting and flirting, that cockroaches rarely mate in love.

Judy's thesis, in the process of being ultimated, was titled: *Cockroaches can be taught to run mazes and can even learn some things when decapitated.*

I laughed again.

"The train?"

"The train."

She went to Philadelphia looking for Morris Elliot, the mandril astronomer, a Gemini, who lived on a river and used to go canoeing with Guido O. Shait, my supposed alter ego.

For the record, I have to say that Morris was one of a band of distinguished astronomers who contended that the evolution of the universe and, in particular, the formation of galaxies, had greatly depended upon a series of catastrophic explosions. And he was right. Contemporary evidence, arrived at through x-rays, suggests that seismic waves derived from such catastrophic explosions initiated the formulation of galaxies, and one of those waves presumably created the sun and the planets about 4.5 billion years ago. And more so, he had a theory about the quasars — those mysterious beacons of radiation in the far sky. Quasars, he would say, are the cores of galaxies, and black holes are the energy that push quasars. When a quasar dies out, a black hole remains in the galaxy. Black holes, ultimately, are products of gravitational collapse: matter so densely embroidered that light cannot escape its pull. He specu- lated that supermassive black holes can be present in active or ordinary galaxies such as M32 and An- dromeda.

As for G.O., he was a good architect, a would be painter and a would-be actor who, in spite of himself, appeared in *The Twelfth Macaque.* He was a sinuous and gossamer-like Scorpio with a head of curly hair in the ancient Roman style, much sought after and patron- ized. I never liked him.

I phoned Lisa and right off the bat I asked her if her night had been free of remorse and regrets.

Angrily she replied: "I woke up drenched. But all I saw were a man's arms. And they weren't yours."

Another gentle Lisa's phantom fucks, I told myself. Then I asked:

"Did you recognize them?"

"They were G.O.'s, maybe . . . "

"Guido?"

"They were strong and long. A hand was missing."

"So!"

I did not know how but I got disheartened on the phone. My eyes were burning now. I was not shedding tears, but I squeezed them shut for an instant. G.O. came into my darkness, luminous, observing me with his seductive smile.

Guido's girl-students especially adored him. He talked to them about art in terms of Zen and exhorted them to patience, tenacity in planning, and total fidelity to ideals. Often he discoursed on carnal love — not so much as to no longer desire it or look for it — but always with the detachment and melancholy air of one who is an expert on the subject.

One morning, seven years ago, precisely at the be- ginning of the academic year, a girl, dressed only in her nightgown, climbed up to the platform of her dormitory and leaped into the void. They said that she had taken LSD. It was also said that she had been forsaken by, or disappointed with, Professor Shait. It caused him enormous suffering, above all because the story wasn't true.

"She posed for me once, but I never finished that nude. She was a strange girl. One night she stood behind the door of my studio and waited all night for me to open it. But she had not knocked and I didn't know that she was outside my door and, anyway, it's always open. In the morning, when I set out for school, I found her there almost frozen to death. In the car I warmed her with my hands. But who could imagine that she was so crazy?"

G.O. Shait was an unhappy person. He betrayed friendship unwittingly, and lied to himself just as unwittingly. He was fully convinced, however, that his presence in the world was essential, while all other things and persons that danced around him were accessories.

To base art on sex was wrong from the start. To use art for sex was amusing but it was illusionistic and likewise did not hold water from the start. To view art as an escape from individual shortcomings or physical handicaps was a forgivable fraud, as illness in an individual was forgivable. But it was enormously embarrassing when it created illness in the other and coinvolved the other and asked the other for further forgiveness. Art and love revealed themselves in a flash, but both had deep roots in the unconscious. They lasted for such a brief spell that the one who picked up the pieces would be lacerated forever by a feeling of insufficiency and vindication. Such things were not my cup of tea, but they certainly appertained to Guido because he was an unhappy person.

One day, while building a house, he sawed off his hand. The right eye, perfect when he was painting, did not see the saw which was the task of the left eye to see. He was building ordinary houses out of rejects, empty tomato cans, beer bottles, and pressed card board. They were intimate and exotic, and he sold them. Thanks to his meticulous patience G.O. had managed to achieve a respectable financial situation. It was accompanied by artistic distance, a melancholy raging passion for psychedelic experiences, and a never-ending quest for sexual ecstasies sewn together by threads of mysticism.

He picked his hand out of the dust and placed it on a brick. His skinny and sad-looking mastiff, Rhin-Thin-Stone sniffed the bloody hand, toyed with it and then ate it in one gulp. G.O. beat the dog savagely on that rage-filled afternoon, and for twelve nights and thirteen days he lay moaning on the withered and compassionate breast of his wife, Sphinx.

Over the phone I said to Lisa: "Look here now, our infidelities are reciprocal."

"Have you seen Rose?"

"Judy's been here."

"But wasn't she supposed to be in New Orleans?"

"She was. But at this moment she's en route to Philadelphia, looking for Morris Elliot who is canoeing with your 'Cropped-hand.'"

She suddenly became silent. I knew her so well: her mind ran back to episodes of the past, to things that we had done individually and which, subsequently, we recounted to each other because we had established a truth pact between us.

This was our only freedom. It served us as a seductive stimulus to lofty ideals, a weapon of aggressiveness in both our public and private deficiencies, a basis for deductive conclusions, and a warming, coddling baby blanket.

We did not have an "open" marriage, which can be possible only without jealousy (which is never possible), but we insisted on truth as a summons to order, especially during agonizing sexual desires and during their eventual realization, after which we told each other about the particulars, lustrous or shabby, and about our perverse fantasies. It beguiled us into wanting still to be together, scratching and martyring each other, which we endured because we were proud of our reciprocal sado-masochism. We did build our glass house with the pure intent to be pure. But now it reflected the outrageous sides of our muddy personalities. It was our mirror-image house and we the adolescents living in it.

We used truth, above all, as a form of seduction because we knew that now nobody really seduced anybody, as innocence no longer had any value whatsoever.

A phrase commonly heard among middle-aged academics (unlucky enough to have neo-Ph.D. wives who always looked like nineteen year olds in search of forbidden coition) was the following: "Well . . . all that is involved is an interesting interlude."

Interlude, that is, a conjugal parenthesis, an esoteric and diversifying mini-passion which neither overwhelmed nor lingered for long, and which even included subsequent tears and pardons and readmission of the fugitives to the bourgeois cage. This was obviously wrong because the interesting interlude inevitably led to but one port: separation, half lives, other lives. It was a lethal, miasma-soaked game. Sex experienced in this way was a swamp. Period. Nevertheless, we decided to continue the game and possibly to extend it up to the next day or up to the new winter. It was painful, of course. Even this was something else: It was the price to be paid and it remained absolutely personal, totally devoid of any interest to others, since love's pain was real and the pursuit of happiness, in which everybody was engaged, was an illusion. We needed illusions in order to live.

At the same time will entered into a new channel. That of psychosomatic dysfunction. A form of illness that grew in the shadow of the energy contained in the illusion. The illusion preserved us niveously. The basic dysfunction ultimately cut off our legs. But that had been written: so we wouldn't end up in a peal of laughter, like those great writers who, at the close of a career, turned to humor.

Question: Were you really thinking that a factual physical illness was taking possession of you, Simon, as a result of an already conscious psychological dysfunction?

Question: Didn't you deal with the subject in several clinical psychological articles, in which you substantiated how a disturbance occasioned by a social or political event — marriage, divorce, mourning, retirement — can often be the cause of the physical illness, such as cancer, cardiac collapse, hypertension, morbid daredevilism, and in your case, the motorcycle?

Question: Have you ever thought of submitting yourself to R.H. Rabe and G.W. Brown for verification of your disturbances?

"Okay, Simon," Lisa exclaimed. "I'm sorry I didn't get to see her. How was she?"

"Feverish."

"It's all Punks' fault, leaving her without a cent."

"He couldn't help it!"

"Do you agree with me?"

"Nooo!"

"Why?"

"You women always talk about economics before and after the betrayal, and it's always the husband or the lover who must pay for your frailty because he desires you, because he possesses you, because he marries you. Don't you know that Judy is tortured only by her sex? Punks showed me a list of a long series of occasional lovers whom she still visits regularly, often twice a day, every day. How is Punks to be blamed for that?"

"But he's the sex-tortured one, not Judy. And you're just like him. Both understand each other perfectly," she retorted, raising her voice.

Lowering mine, I continued: "And wake up like her, right? Whereas I continue to represent the religious, familial phallus, the sharp-edged stone protecting the entrance to the cave."

"And how about Evelyn and Rose," she shouted, hanging up.

I was utterly upset again, holding the open telephone in my hand, my eyes fixed on a lecture schedule. I thought wearily to myself: She'll be pouncing on me like a bolt out of the blue demanding reparations in the form of sex and caresses for twenty-four hours. She will force me to neglect my work, telephone calls, unpaid bills, lectures to be prepared, shopping, and the laundry.

Believe it or not, Simon does everything around the house.

The Pisces woman was a pendant on the penis. And this pendant had almost entirely devoured mine.

4

Suddenly she was back from New Canaan, standing in the driveway threshold, looking angry and breathless, only three hours after the phone call, as if she had been literally running all the way. I noticed a new dent on the car.

"What's this?"

"I banged into another car in a parking lot. I also got stopped for speeding."

With a fatherly air, I remarked: "Speeding is pure, if it's intensified by terror."

"I'm not terrorized."

"Of course you are. You've got your second ticket. One more and they'll take away your license. And one fine day they'll also bust you and lock you up in a tiny cell without window panes and TV, and I'll come to visit you bearing small baskets of red tomatoes along with wicked, little erotic letters in which I'll tell you all about love."

I drew closer and kissed her on the neck, chastely. She clung to me and the closeness relaxed her.

"What smells so nice? A new perfume?"

"Caron. I bathed myself in it to draw the attention of the cops."

"One of these days you'll also draw the attention of a ravine or a telephone pole. I will weep and weep inconsolably, and bring baskets of tomatoes to place on your grave bearing the photograph of an angel on the headstone, and I'll declaim Andromaca's position to you."

"You're beautiful, Simon. Play with my skull."

"Hell, no! I'll be Mercury. All alone and thrice one. Because it is I who impregnates, generates, gives birth, devours, kills . . . even myself."

Dancing, I made my way to the oven-like brick kitchen adjoined to the glass house. I grabbed a basket of red tomatoes and carried it into the Pearls Gate. Then I went out to the garden and gathered some red roses, and took them into the room. Finally, I went out to my study across the meadow and brought back an acrylic painting which I myself made of her: a sweet face with an enigmatic smile, covered by enormous sunglasses. Her amulet, two fish darting in opposite directions, hung from her neck. They were reflected in her sunglasses transformed into two enormous male members, one in a state of erection, the other in decline. I then arranged a mini altar on the chest of glass drawers. I went into the kitchen once more and returned with two candlesticks which I lit in front of the painting.

"Are you crazy?"

"I've prepared the altar."

I took a red tomato from the basket and placed it on the palm of her hand. Amused, he accepted it silently, examining. Then she suddenly bit into it, squirting the red juice over her milk-white neck.

"I suppose that's the way you'd like to eat me, spilling blood."

"No, come, let's suffer together. Would you like to?"

"In this room?"

"Isn't this the room where you brought Judy? What did you do to her?"

"Oh, I see what you're driving at."

She liked to hear gruesome and macabre tales. They formed part of a ritual at the beginning of the Jade banquet.

"I bound her to the bed, hand and foot," I said, "and I tickled her like that old pig Karamazov. You remember that dirty old man Karamazov, of course."

"No, I don't know," she says, perplexed.

"Judy, however, survived," I guffawed, remembering her cockroaches.

We tumbled onto the bed, already in the throes of a burgeoning anxiety. But, as if we were in an empty glass tomb all we heard was the echo of our own laughter, a distant whistling in our ears, and the insect-like crackling of the waning wax on the candelabra.

"You also brought Evelyn here," she said. "And it is also here that you brought Rose. It's always here that you carry out your vendettas. Now look upon me not as your Lisa but as someone else, a stranger, and amuse me. Why don't you dance for me?"

"Okay . . . I'm Pithagoras. I'm Nijinsky . . . I can even dance for you . . . But why me?" I said in a sudden brusque tone of voice. "Why don't you dance for me? You use me and consume me. Even your dreams give you away."

"What dreams?"

"Come off it, love. You know perfectly well that your betrayals are as specific as mine. Listen, just listen to me. Why don't we try to rediscover ourselves? I mean to say . . . beyond this farce?"

"Impossible! We've known each other for fourteen years. And the new is always strange, never familiar."

"Granted."

"Tell me a story, Dad. Tell me all about the past."

"How would you like to hear the one about the Dwarf and the Girl with the basket of red tomatoes?"

"You, of course, are the Dwarf and I'm the Girl, right?"

"The other day, walking through a patch of woods, a girl with a basket of red tomatoes came upon a dwarf who wanted to gobble her up. Where are you going, pretty girl? To my grandmother who is ill . . . Oh my dear, dear girl! I who am famished come before your grandmother. Come, I'll take you to my lair and you can sleep there. No, no, Mr. Dwarf, I'll sleep with my grandmother. Her arms are tender, while yours are big and hairy. So they are, child. But you also have big teeth, Mr. Dwarf. Oh, my dear child, don't you know that strong teeth bite better? The girl didn't at all know that it was dangerous to come across a dwarf."

"But I love you, Dwarf."

"No, you don't. You're about to run away, Princess."

"I tell you I'm undressing."

I helped her to undress, ritualistically, hurling one piece of clothing here and another there. We acted out our sickness.

"Wait a moment," I said. "I'll put a rock record on."

Since in cases of extreme depravation moralism almost reinforces the depravation, I began my moralizing tale which amused her.

"Look here," I said. "Our life is really droll, a sad joke. It's two-faced: a face we put on for the outside, for others; and one fixed for the inside, for you and for me. On the outside we are social saints, and inside our own glass house we are monsters, prisoners of perverted habits, voluntary suicides for the lack of sincerity with ourselves."

"It's not true, it's not true! But if you want to leave me, just do. Go ahead! In fact, I'll leave you first by planting a bomb in the garage."

"Exactly. Just as Judy would like to do with Punks. Boommm!"

I said that laughing and it made her laugh too. I wonder why. Moralism, how troublesome! So I thought of my mother. But why?

My mother, a Quebecois Catholic, wanted me to become a priest or a missionary. And my father, a Jew without a synagogue, wanted me to become a rabbi. He had converted to Christianity to escape the sentence passed on the Chosen People to set up house and store in every angle of the world from which they then were to be expelled, and thus remain permanently at the mercy of the event of Exodus. We Donas, a heraldic family of Selimo, changed our name and social station in order to better defend our right to non-assimilation. Knowing this, I avoided synagogue and monastery alike, but in the fury of deciding I blindly ended up in the war and, of course, on the wrong side. I was finally saved thanks to the intercession of Eloi, our super protector, who had a white beard reaching down to his knees. Through his Neapolitan messenger, Professor Anacleto Zinghelli, he immediately acquainted me with the sad fable about a son and a father.

A father teaches his son, still a toddler, to be more courageous. He sets him down on a step and invites him to jump, assuring him that he will catch him in mid-air in his arms. After a moment's hesitation, the child makes the leap and ends up in his father's arms. But precisely when the boy makes his last and highest leap, the father deliberately moves out of reach and the son falls flat on his face. At the very moment that he is picking himself up, aching and astonished, the father pitilessly makes his son aware of the truth he wants to pass on to him: "Thus, you will learn not to trust a cauliflower, even if it's your father."

But Eloi, our super protector, still opened his arms protectingly and welcomingly to me. And it was at this point that he let me know that I should grow, rebelling perhaps even against him, because at my next mistake I would most certainly be alone, without a past and without a primary trust.

After absorbing the moral of the story, I began to roam all over the world. I was now a scientist. At the middle of that wandering I found myself wearing an academic cap and gown *ad honorem,* one could say, precisely in recognition of those voyages I made, those researches I conducted, those books I wrote, those international conferences I attended, those diplomas I received, those medals I was awarded, those monkeys I saved. Nevertheless, death pays me a visit every fifteen years, punctually.

At age twenty came the resurrection after death in the Italian Civil War. At age thirty-five came my resurrection in America, after death in my native Selimo. And now, on the threshold of fifty, comes the new shattering blow that draws near. I am so conscious of witnessing myself dying it inebriates me with a new life.

Now there was an old man who danced in a room which had the form of a pit or a womb, as well as of a grotto where miracles were performed. The only reality was the shadow of the clown reflected on the glass walls by the flame of the candles. There was a knife in the tinydrawer of the glass night table. The old man reached for it, felt the thin blade under his fingers, stuck it in his mouth and then removed it and hurled it on the wooden floor where she, Lisa, was an enormous spot of fear.

She cut her feet, traced lines of blood, the room filled up with red tomatoes, she wept and laughed, knelt in front of him and bit him with her sharp, greedy, grating teeth, beating him with her open palms, after which they rolled up together on the mattress, after which they rolled up together in the moldy dust under the bed.

"You're really crazy, Simon."

"How about yourself, Princess?"

"I'm a wreck, a desperate one, Simon. And I'm going to lose you."

"It also applies to you, dear baby. Soon you will walk alone, and you will be more splendid than ever."

"I don't understand, I don't understand you anymore, Simon."

"Do you remember *The Twelfth Macaque?* Its message was that life, earthly and eternal alike, that of God and that of God and men and women are based on two opposites: light/shadow, good/evil, love/betrayal, father/son . . . And the film also speaks of growth, becoming. You, too, will have to grow, suffer, and die."

"Stop it, you frighten me!"

"The two of us will be losers. But the work of betrayal is identified with the work of redemption. Isn't it possible that we may be looking for something definitive?"

"But what are you looking for?" She picked the knife up from the floor and placed it against my chest. "Explain yourself, once and for all time, or I'll kill you!"

"You've already done so!"

She threw the knife away and started to cry all over again.

32

"We will die of sorrow, Princess. But don't worry, I'll build you the new house anyway, as promised. And I'll have G.O. design it. It will be a tunnel. And when you're weary of that house too, and gone away, I will become completely mute and spend my time sewing dolls and listening to Eddie Lang on my master tapes, or waiting for you to phone to tell me all about your new lover."

"Lover?" She arched herself, suddenly curious. "What's my lover like, Daddy? Would you describe him, please?"

"He's tall and unhappy like all lovers. He's an anti-hero, but he still likes to run around the gym and lift weights."

"Are you referring to your counterfigure, G.O.?"

"You yourself have mentioned his name."

"But you drive me to saying things, you drive me to doing things. What do you want from me?"

"One of these days you'll abandon Daddy and you will become Eve. Eve is already preformed in the Garden, and the Serpent already exists in the Garden."

"Is G.O. the serpent?"

"I haven't said it. Again you yourself have mentioned him. But listen. A christologist, Mario Brelich, claims that the serpent is Chaos, that is, the undifferentiated as such, which does not have a will of its own like a person or like God, but acts according to its internal laws. It is Evil. And it is Evil because it is the opposite of Good which is Order, Light. But it does not wish Evil, because it wishes nothing. It tempts man only because man gives in to the temptations of Chaos. And the serpent, like Satan, is he who is not, the one who, at the same time, could be all. His wickedness is innate, natural to his essence, to his nonexistent will. Now do you understand what Evil is?"

"I'm sleepy."

"So am I."

They swallowed the pill and slept for ten hours. When they awoke a full moon was obnoxiously spying amid the trees beyond the meadow. They got down on each other with leathery tongues and fell asleep for another three hours. He was on a bridge where the brook disappears. She was now wearing the transparent tunic of dreams and was slowly waking up. Even the sun seemed to be lying in wait. All that was left of the moon was a vague remembrance, stamped in the air like an empty circle.

Indeed everything was really a dream, Simon. "You're torturing this poor girl! But for heaven's sake, don't stop! Torture becomes her."

"Listen, Lisa, this is the monologue," I said.

Sitting up on the bed, looking lean and stunned, I placed a hand on her shoulder, after which I placed my shoulder on her shoulder, and gazed at the surrounding woods, the sun through the foliage. But Lisa yawned, and I started talking:

"You've never had a wife in Lisa Jones. First, you had a daughter, then a piece of luggage to carry here and there, to be open and shut at will, to love or reject at will. Later, you had a semi-adult woman with a flat and embroidered pussy, with tiny immaculate tits. She was trying to write a thesis on Joyce's *Dubliners*, met the circle of your friends, started to form a circle of her own friends, and now she looks at the world on behalf of self, exclusively.

"You wanted a family? You just weren't made for that. Family is capitalism, a concept that originated in your Italy with Leon Battista Alberti's *Della famiglia,* at the base of which is *virtù,* namely the ability to control your own fortune. With marriage love becomes a contract (see Spenser). Love is no longer tragic, but domesticated. Have you ever wanted a family?

"Yes. You wanted to construct a capitalist corporation in the name of children and of the dowry. But you have never loved, or am I mistaken? Not even yourself. This is why you possess yourself, and this is why you possess this poor little girl. You've married your daughter instead, raping her in the park. Is this the reason of your illness? Or are there other reasons?

"Yes, glaucoma, your glaucomic look.

"You see more and want more because you know that soon you will not see at all. That's why you look at the wet panties of hysterical little girls searching for a father. This is how you ensnared this eternal girl student, your wife, and this is why you built a glass house, your own vault. You're horrible!"

Lisa yawned. She went to the brick cylinder with a bathroom inside and, sitting on the pot, smoked her first cigarette of the day, looking as thin and worn out as Virginia Woolf at eighteen.

She started reading the horoscope.

You too went to the brick cylinder and sat on the pot beside her, just as kings and queens used to in the old times of romance.

"You know, Princess? To conquer a Pisces woman is not a difficult enterprise. This is said by Lucia Alberti, a Viennese astrologer living in Rome. For the Pisces woman is so easily influenced. She thinks so emotionally, so distant from reality. The fact that she lives in a world of her own invention makes her see in you a man of unsurpassable qualities, the richest, the handsomest, the most intelligent of the world, even if you are just a state employee with a smattering of humanistic culture.

"Unfortunately, you are not this person, Simon, but the man who will come, who will tenderly touch Lisa's delicate skin, and who will talk to you about solipsism and nature, about psychedelic experiences and about EST."

"EST. EST. EST, yes?"

"Dear love! He is coarse and shy, choleric and querulous, and likes very much the duplicitous life in which elegance is maintained and poverty shown off."

"Not you?"

"Actually, he has no reason for a betrayal. He's simply the one who reaches out an arm and grabs."

"G.O., I know!"

"On the contrary, you, Simon, have so many possible reasons for letting yourself be betrayed. You are looking for death, Simon; whereas the other is not interested in death although he, too, will die with sorrow. But he will be gentle with you. He will transfigure you, he will have you get a nose-job, he will have you redye your hair, seeking the natural root in you, he will dress you in blue jeans, he will put the generative cross around your neck, the cross of fertility, though he's an impotent. G.O. is your prefabricated type, you see that? The difference between him and me is this: He's gentle and I'm rude. He's shy and I'm one who walks among monkeys."

"You're only too crazy."

"No, Simon. You die for her. Or, better, you don't. You're a misogynist. You like the company of men or to be alone, writing of your discoveries, whereas you would like the woman around you only to dry your wet feet, to fuck, to have children, and to do house work, in short a woman as convenience and fate. You are frighteningly childish, Simon. Or is it all because of the glaucoma?"

"Yes, oh yes! You're frighteningly childish, Simon," she screamed and pulled the chain.

I, the idiot, ran after her in the meadow. I grabbed her and jerked her naked shoulders, yelling: "Go, Lisa! Go find your happiness."

"I'm happy with you," she said, and started to whine.

5

I have always been enamored of clouds. One of them, Judy Madison, crouches herself on my head and carries me off. I'm alone. I'm perfectly alone. Yet memory continues to make something of the past surface to consciousness, and offers me the continuity of time.

The remembrance involves lots of smoke, lots of laughter, lots of critiques following the screening of the film short, *The Twelfth Macaque*. Now the remembrance encompasses the ritual celebration in Judy and Andrew's house on South Black Lake Road, with the usual friends, professors, couples, husbands and wives, husbands without wives, wives without husbands, who are exploring and querying each other, a rattling world of divorcées, a teeming world à la Magritte, unctuous, sticky, tense as a tightrope, hysterical, made of sex and hedonism, a rather ambiguous and difficult sport of aesthetic pleasure which my friends engage in with a weary arrogance.

The screening of the film was followed by some rather important critical comments. But soon it became a clash of opinions between opposed and hated cliques of professors, pederasts, lesbians, supercritics, christologists, and racists. Some said the film was an attack on women, others said it was a defense of women and homosexuality. Others, still, contended that it was an attack on gossip-mongering and the defective academic world.

All expounded and defended their theses, but nobody had clear ideas, not even the two academicians who had made the film, Madison and Dona. The presentation by the philosopher Anacleto Zinghelli confounded ideas even more and promoted bitter resentments. Zinghelli, an authority on Manzoni and Lope de Vega, had a Jesuit past and had published a series of articles on christology which had led to his ouster from the Church as a heretic, an event which subsequently destroyed his whole life.

The fifty-five-year-old Zinghelli, today a father of two children, had obtained a doctorate in theology at a young age at the Gregorian University of Rome, following which he left on a mission to Brazil. Although he was very devout and fervent as regards the precepts of Holy Mother Church, he had committed an *autodafé* with a little book on christology, titled *The Hermeneutic Circle of the Gospels*. Since the 1950s, when the Rev. Zinghelli was writing from Brazil, all biblical scholars, apart from fundamentalists, thought that the Gospels were not objective documentation of chronological events, but rather the result of an ambivalent play between historical events and their interpretation by the first believers. On the one hand, the contemporaries of Jesus deduced his life from their remembrances when, after the Paschal feast, they interpreted the significance of his glorification and his awaited return while, on the other hand, their post-Paschal faith formed their interpretation of his historical life.

The excommunication went to him with the words, *Roma locuta est, causa finita est*. Rome has spoken, the case is closed.

From that day on Anacleto was called *Ananas* by his male friends. He was a frail, stocky man. And for the occasion he did not sit on the desk of the Lecture Center 7 but on the lectern surmounting the desk. He spoke in a strident yet booming voice, and it was not exactly clear whether he was speaking in English or Italian, Portuguese or Hebrew. However, each one of the auditors understood him in his/her own language. Many laughed out of scorn; others from disappointment.

He concluded by saying that "this absurd story of a man who fails to understand that love is not possession, that a vagina is a great all-embracing mother made to receive all her children, all the penises of this world, and in particular the penises of traitors; this absurd story of hearts exulcerated in the crucible of Accademia, of penises rendered impotent by the affront suffered, takes on the color and contour of beauty, and is transmuted into a kind of aurora borealis. It becomes a conjunction of kings, an alchemic opus from which is born a deeper truth, in which the Shadow also has its role . . . "

Then he went back to sit in a chair next to Andrew and me, and Andrew murmured in his ear:

"You've certainly tired yourself out while attempting to destroy us."

Zinghelli shook his head in denial.

"*Incertus animus dimidium est sapientiae.* Half of my wisdom is uncertain mind," he translated. And suddenly he looked sad as if asking himself, "What did I do that wasn't right?"

It was modish at that time to quote from Latin or Greek and even from Provençal. Different academics, Dona and Zinghelli among them, translated from Terence, Seneca, Publius Sirus, and Ovid. Dionigi translated from the Greek. It was always irritating to interpolate a discussion with a Latin phrase to Latinless academics. A favorite with Zinghelli and myself was Publius Sirus, a mimeographer of the times of Caesar and Cicero, famous above all for his gnomic utterances written in iambic and trochaic verse. What wasn't right was that he was boring stiff with quotations and much, much malice.

The eyes of a few persons sought out Guido and often fixed their gaze on Lisa's ashen face.

Lisa was sitting next to Judy and Charlotte Shark, the redoubtable lady professor of linguistics. She was known to everybody only as the cutting edge of the Seagulls Movement, but she threw her weight around primarily as the brains of the academic Inner Circle in which the political power was centralized.

Charlotte, however, studied pigeons instead of seagulls, convinced that one day they would be able to learn a series of symbols and through them commit themselves to speech. She followed certain theories on environmental behavior suggested by the psychologist B.F. Skinner, and dismissed the more sensible analyses offered by Chomsky, a legitimate linguist, who contends that human language is a specific biological system that has developed through millions of years. Hence, the first rudiments of speech cannot be the result of a particular environment.

Charlotte had a nice appearance, but she eternally dressed as a male and wore half-length boots. She was athletic, her laughter was frank, her speech proper, and she gave the impression of having been a voracious reader. The truth of the matter, however, was only one: She was power-mad and vindictive to the point of hysteria. From Skinner she had learned that animals can be conditioned, and once they have learned to execute orders they are to be rewarded. She employed the club and carrot tactic, and a lashing humor.

I was a target of it, just like any other chauvinist pig in Accademia.

My middle name was Gionata, or Jonathan, son of Saul and friend of David (in the Old Testament), but Charlotte called me Simon-Jona, perhaps to annoy me. Obviously, this was a reference to Jonah who, as the Old Testament says, survived for three days in the whale's belly and who decided to accomplish his assigned mission only after he was vomited onto the beach. But Charlotte also called me *Corvo di Salaparuta,* because of my fondness for that Sicilian wine which I had sent to me from Italy in small cases. And, in return, I did not forget to carve for her a splendid piece in my film.

In *The Twelfth Macaque,* the principal characters were dressed as monkeys, chimpanzees, or humanoids, as I had devised an allegorical and moralistic form for my subject. I derived its structure primarily from a medieval play on the seven capital sins, later embellishing it in the manner of a fabulist modeled on Carlo Gozzi, author of *The Love of the Three Oranges* (1777). Charlotte figured in it as man/woman and was assigned the role of Death.

There were of course other actors: Peter, Matthias, Rafael, Dionigi, Morris, Jack, Carmen, Bartholomew, and Guido. But almost nobody knew Guido as Guido, because his name had been reduced to a monogram: G.O.

He was there with his wife Sphinx, next to Bart and Cara, directly behind the rows of seats occupied by Judy, Lisa, and Charlotte. Further down, in Guido's row, sat Fat Jack and his young chauffeur-lover, Bob, and still further down sat Dionigi, over whom his wife,

Blanche, wielded a firm, heavy, and beringed hand. Matthias and Morris who, for awhile, had been leaning against the exit door opened it surreptitiously and sneaked away.

The moderator, Sonny Morebugs, an enthusiast of Finnish sauna, took note of Charlotte's upraised hand and invited her to speak.

She rose from her seat and made her way to the platform in her inseparable yoke-yellow boots matching the rest of her dress. She labeled the film "a comic operetta on hedonism," with a particular emphasis on sacrifice. But whose sacrifice? Of which macaque, the Thirteenth? The Betrayer or the Savior? And who would be the traitor, Guido? Guido in the skin of a gray Hanu man languor, named for the monkey god of the Ramayana? Who would be the redeemer, I, Simon-Jona? I, Simon in the skin of the uncatchable "wild lion-tailed macaque with a tufted tail and a bushy mane?" Who is finally killed with a shot from the carbine of the character symbolizing Envy, who is in the service of Death? "The biblical nuances are obvious," said Charlotte, "but from the Text — the Screen — they appear to be of a blasphemous and desacralizing nature."

She then turned to the subject of hedonism and attempted a definition: It was a subtle vice that insinuated itself with tacit fraud. In art its purpose was practical rather than aesthetic. It fondled and stimulated that area of light and shade lying between spirit and sense.

"Both Simon-Jona and Andrew," Charlotte added, "by parodying the mores and customs of academic society wanted to derive something romantic and adventurous from a schematic plot. They have made a film of content, based on a rich series of orgies and various erotic performances, embroidering with a subtle perfidy the biblical idea underlying the subject: namely, Betrayal as Rebirth. The hidden thesis of this film suggests, in a pornotheological form, that love is inexorably linked to our personal crucifixion. Eve, like Guido, will betray us in the very act in which she approaches us to plant a kiss on our lips. Yet without Eve, life is naught else but a cruel game played by children tumbling down staircases. Love is self-love because betrayal exists, and life is life because death exists. Hardly a great revelation!"

"I would add," interjected Ananas Zinghelli, "that God is God because Satan exists, and Jesus is Jesus because Judas exists."

"I'm really sorry," retorted Charlotte.

6

Everybody was at the party, even Charlotte. She continued to discuss the film from her viewpoint, at first with Anacleto Zinghelli, the fiercest critic of the Administration which, benignly, had never retaliated, and then with Barth Bellicapelli, an authority on the Mafia, whose major interest was to gather and redistribute (after his personal revision) intelligence data on the academic Inner Circle. A motto dear to Alphonse Bertillon hung on the door of his office: "One can see only what one observes, and one observes only the things already in his mind."

Charlotte had once made a stylistic study of Barth's novels, which were quite well known in the film world and in CIA circles. She defined them as "exercises in hedonistic literature to be ranked between the psychologism of James and the abnormal and decadent predilections of the esoteric Huysmans."

At this point Charlotte drew Barth's attention to the fact that "this film is a product of the will to power in sexually impotent authors."

"Oh, no, not at all!" Barth replied, laughing. "It's just a game being played by two guys who want to free themselves of their respective wives."

A point should be made. The Seagull Movement and anti-sexuality often went arm in arm. Although lust was equally strong in man and woman with the result that both sexes were preoccupied with sex, sexual freedom was not sufficient to neutralize woman's power in sexual transactions. A whole ancient and contemporary ritual documented that among all peoples it was generally the man who courted, proposed, seduced, used gifts in exchange for sex, and availed himself of the service of harlots. And the thesis of scholars such as Blau, Malinowski, Siskind, and Symonds demonstrated that modern feminism did not appear to be anti-sexual, yet contemporary seagull writings on female sexuality emphasized masturbation and, frequently, lesbianism which (in a certain sense) are political equivalents of anti-sexuality.

Charlotte and her group, therefore, saw in "hedonistic" literature an action on the part of males that simultaneously revealed and restricted female supremacy in sexual transactions.

G.O. was also at the party. Charlotte contended that he imitated Gustave Moreau and drew phallic flowers in the manner of Josephin Péladan. G.O. was his usual gentle and subtle self. He chastely kissed Lisa on the forehead and Simon square on the mouth, tonguing him lightly.

"What am I to call this," I protested in utter disbelief, "the kiss of Guido?"

We all laughed, but Sphinx shook her head, looking worried.

Morris Elliot was also present. He was a man with tiny, very blue eyes, with curly hair, with a crooked nose like that of the Duke of Urbino, and his thin lips easily expanded into a smile suspended somewhere between irony and fear. He dressed like the generic executive type, and when he showed up at gatherings he never greeted anyone in particular, sat down anywhere, and suddenly began to speak in fits and starts, usually about a trivial happening, after which he just as unceremoniously took his leave for an ever unknown destination. He screwed Judy in his office while the students were stretched out in the corridor, in front of the door, waiting for it to be opened and for him to appear at the door, his chin looking more withered than ever, a sign that he was ready to resume his interminable seminar on the black holes of the universe.

Judy Madison's heterosexual and sophisticated oddities were of such a kind and quantity that some of them had leaked out to the male world. Simon Dona, in his talks to the selected, trusted few, often compared the sexual prowess of this woman with her Mangaian or Polynesian model-counterpart. Judy subjected her partners to an intensive sexual investigation, testing their virility and masculinity, their gift-giving and courtship practice, before they were granted access to the moist charms of her *inner sanctum.*

Punks, her husband, was not annoyed by her kinkiness, but he was decidedly weary of it and already giving some thought to changing career and mate alike. Indeed, he transmitted this weariness to Simon, even though the latter had always believed himself strongly attracted by Judy's aberrations. Perhaps there were more truth than wit in Barth's remark: "It's just a game being played by two guys who want to free themselves of their respective wives."

In addition to Matthias, Dionigi, Carmen and their wives, also present were Fat Jack and Bob, Roland and Kate DeCee with King Priapus who makes love to Kate in his sauna with Roland's permission. Larry and Williamina Fourdays were also there. Larry weaved in and out among the couples, patting female asses. He started his patting procedure with Lisa, moved on to Blanche, Dionigi's wife, then to Williamina who was trying to interest Roland in her belly, no longer tautly adolescent, and finally to Judy who had just made her entry and stretched herself out on the divan in front of the fireplace, resting her little curled head like a puff on my slumbering cock.

The voices that were heard here and there were commenting on Charlotte's critique, remembering now that the death of the Master had left a void, but one which nobody really felt anymore.

WILLIAMINA: No, he was not a real humanist. He didn't give a damn about people.

ROLAND: Not for man as he has existed up to now, but for man in the making.

LARRY: But he opposed his own influence. He considered literature to be bourgeois, and repeated, "I write. It's my vice, but it doesn't feed hungry children." He said that political commitment was all, and asked to be forgiven for writing.

BLANCHE: If I were to reduce his thesis to a single sentence, I would say that "the subconscious is structured like a language." And who knows what it means? Is it linked to the new religiosity, anti-rational, anti-scientific, anti-positive? "Try to be impossible" are among its slogans.

WILLIAMINA: Yes, we are making a return to a tolerance of different points of view which we thought had been lost forever. Yes, there's really been a clean break.

All the guests left, except for Lisa and myself (and by chance Zinghelli, curled up on the floor in a dark corner). The lights went out, and a slight grudge against everything somehow clung to us, but we chose to defer for the time being.

The smoke had had an hallucinatory effect on all our minds, but the effect seemed also to be boredom.

In fact, Judy observed: "Boredom is heat."

"This film is the beginning of the end," I replied.

"Of Accademia or of us?"

"Of us, of you, of them, what do I know?"

"We'll also keep on going along separate paths," Judy said.

The feeling of dullness came from the dullness of the hour, from the cold of the uncurtained window panes that let in the night, from the heat that warms the central part of my body, from the weight of this tiny head that is obscurely arousing the worm lying in ambush. She rubbed her face against it, then she reached out a hand to grab mine, which was inert, and transferred it from her tit to her twat which was flat and throbless but I also knew that naked it was crude, wild, and fruitless.

Suddenly I became aware of Lisa's absence. But I didn't make a move. I tried to survey the surveyable corners of the room from the corner of my eye. Lisa was in a corner with Andrew, chair against chair, leg against leg, face against face, like two porcelain statues hanging on a wall. Lisa was smiling. a doltish Gioconda, and there was a glint of slyness in Andrew's gleaming eye. Then I heard them get up like two feathers, descending the stairs and entering the room below.

"You stay here," Judy murmured, grabbing me.

Minutes later, when the only sound in the semi-darkness came from the fire, she unzipped me, touched my penis, now poised upright, and gently sunk her head into it.

"You know that's a stupid thing to be doing," I murmured. "Yet it's happening."

"What's happening?"

"Punks and I are swapping wives!"

"It's not your doing or his. It's the wives who want it that way."

When she finished, I got up, fixed my tie, and pulled up my zipper. I felt benumbed and dissatisfied. And I begun to think that there was nothing more pathetic than an unjustified sense of guilt. Nevertheless I felt guilty. And I, too, descended the stairs hesitantly, because I was about to trespass on someone else's turf. The moment I saw her, I barked out the order: "Let's go home, right away!"

"No! Why?" she protested.

They were stretched out on the waterbed, excited and resentful of my intrusion. Judy, too, had appeared in the doorway; she had followed me down the stairs.

"How about the four of us trying that waterbed?" she suggested.

Without further ado she began to strip off her clothes, throwing her dress and bra to one side, and her panties to my face.

"No, no, Simon," Punks protested. "Three's fine, but four's out . . . "

He tried to get on his feet, but he slipped and fell back on the bed.

"The fourth, Andrew, couldn't come because he's ill at home," I said with a sardonic inflection.

To Lisa I simply announced: "I'll wait for you in the car."

She followed me carrying her shoes.

Ananas was huddled up on the back seat of the car like a ball.

"What are you doing here?"

"I'm holding my belly. You have all poisoned me tonight."

On the way back the countryside looked smoothly flowing and luminous.

"Do you like Punks?"

"Very much."

"Would you make it together with him?"

"I've got a date with him tomorrow in the after noon in a motel . . . "

"Which one?"

"The *Scillus Motor Inn*."

"Will you go?"

"I told him no. And you, will you go with Judy?"

"I need something else . . . "

"You need to be less exclusive." And she added: "For the time being you don't have to worry about it. I'll let you know when I'm about to betray you."

"Jesus! What then?" exclaimed Ananas.

Lisa was startled and scared out of her wits. She saw Zinghelli and began to cry. She really wanted to slap his face.

"But what are you doing here? You've heard every-thing . . . "

" . . . and seen everything," I said.

"No, no. Calm down both of you, make love, I won't tell a soul. These things have become common, everybody gets divorces, nothing means anything any more," he said reassuringly. Then he began to laugh, opened the tiny window and stuck his head out. "Night, dear night," he murmured, after which he regaled us with fantastic stories about Brazil, stories suffused with pathos, poverty and extreme oppression which made Lisa weep anew, tears that were all and exclusively hers now, because everything that Zinghelli said disgusted her. Brazil too.

7

Andrew wrote me: *The first one of us that becomes a god will die, mortified by the solitude.*

It was a warning, and I knew it.

Judy and Andrew separated one month later. She took the initiative.

"Why?" I asked Lisa.

"Punks is exclusive."

"Exclusive? In what sense?"

"Like yourself. Whereas Judy is generous."

"Generous? In what sense?"

It was irritating and sarcastic: my irony, her patience.

Then she recited a fable:

"There was once a young husband and a young wife who, before becoming man and wife, had lived together for two years, loving each other intensely and loving intensely whoever they had decided to love: together or separately. They got involved with different persons at the same time that they loved each other, because they wanted to explore all the secrets of sex and of human nature before the nuptial veil and the civil profession. But Punks continued to have friends even afterwards, and Judy did likewise. One fine day Punks brought home one of his laboratory colleagues, Barbara. Do you remember her? The relation became trine. He wanted it so, and the two women submitted.

Judy, however, never got over the shock. From that moment on she sought out other men and other women. And she began to go to the shrink . . . "

"The moral of your fable," I interjected, "seems to be that the Trinity is dangerous!"

Several months later a similar episode happened to us. And the so fatal Number Three was called Rose Spiram. During the lectures I jokingly called her Miss Spiro, Miss Spirito, Miss Soffio, Miss Anemos, Miss Spiramen, Miss Spiritosanto, and so forth and so forth.

Embarrassment and annoyance drove the girl to follow me around at conferences, in the library, in the cafeteria, and in my office where, for some time, even during my absence, she would spend hours seated in a corner, reading my books, doing her homework, oblivious to the coming and going of students and even Lisa's. One day she sarcastically asked her if she had been promoted as my assistant or guardian angel.

"Just what is it that you're looking for, Rose?"

"Me? Nothing."

"You are like my soul, my bad conscience."

"I want to become a nun."

"Why not find yourself a nice boy instead?"

"I had one. He was Sinbad the Sailor. But he died on Prudhoe Bay hunting whales."

"Did they discover oil there?"

"Yes, of course. But he was hunting whales."

"Hunting whales?"

Some years before I had journeyed to the Arctic Polar Circle. From Greenland I moved on to Alaska, visiting Barrow, Prudhoe Bay, Kotsebue, and Nome in bush pilot planes. And often my dreams were people with Eskimos, huskies, bears and caribous. I, too, as a boy, had seen myself as a kind of Sinbad. And now, through her voice, Alaska was coming back to me.

"I would have liked to live in Alaska, but then I would have been sad, very sad," I said.

Without lifting her eyes from the book, she replied:

"I was born in Ketchikan, but they took me away."

Now her people were living in Utica where they owned a small dairy factory and a farm with goats and cows on the Mohawk River. When she returned from her week-end visits home, sometimes she brought back special fresh cheese for her friends. One day she brought back a whole wheel of cheese for me too. Lisa ate most of it.

I advised her to read Jung and see horror movies and to stop bringing me cheese from home and study in her own room or in the library. She replied that Jung was difficult, and that horror movies turned her off. But she stopped coming to the office, to Lisa's relief, and to that of my malevolent colleagues.

One day, however, I found a tiny handmade totem pole on my desk and an envelope that contained a poem she had written. I suddenly realized that the girl had taken a shine to me, and demanded a retribution.

It became clear when she stopped coming to my lectures, she left me to suspect that she had given up the course. I phoned her at the dormitory. She answered that she had not given up the course, but that she was sick.

When teachers become overly protective they expressed themselves as follows:

"Sick? What's the matter? And why didn't you let me know?"

"It's no physical ailment, I'm just homesick for Ketchikan."

"Ah!"

"Yes."

"Is the totem that you left in the office from Ketchikan?"

Surprised, she said:

"It's Chief Johnson's pole, don't you recognize it?"

Why must an anthropologist know everything?

One of my earliest passions had indeed been to study the connection between Christian mythology and the supernatural, as expressed in the totemic figurations of the various Indian people of the Pacific, such as Haida, the Nootka, the Nass, the Tsimsyan, and the Tlingit.

If, on the one hand, totem poles were primarily heraldic monuments in which a family, generally the family of a chief, symbolized the myths that attested its nobility by racing its history and genealogy, on the other hand the myths contained elements that were more super natural than divine in character.

Some poles were carved by Christianized artists and others, like the myth of the Martyr-Bear that recur among the Indians of British Columbia, were used by Missionaries to explain the history and the spirit of Christianity in terms of Indian concepts. In fact, the Pacific Coast Indians have legends which, in addition to Christian elements, we come upon personages and myths with a Mediterranean flavor reminiscent of Orpheus, Prometheus, Samson, and Hercules.

These myths predate the coming of the white man and their similarities with Mediterranean myths suggest the existence of a human myth (Jung's "collective unconscious"), or of "personifications" of needs common to people of all races. But in contrast to the Hebraic-Christian religions according to which man was created in one single day and as being different and superior to the animal, and unlike certain Hinduistic religions which hold that man is equal to the animal, in Indian mythology man is inferior to the animal because the animal is also a spirit.

The animal eludes man with magical arts and, at times, as does the bear, it offers itself to the martyrdom of the hunt for the good and welfare of the people under its protection. The bear transforms itself into man at will, whereas among men only the hero can successfully transmute himself into an animal.

The myth of the Bear-Martyr, in particular, shares similarities with Christianity. The American Indian, as well as the Ural-Altaic peoples of Siberia, call the bear "the grandfather," the "beloved uncle," "the lord," "the godfather." Before the hunt they utter the prayer: "Permit us to kill thee."

The Thompson River Indians address the bear with the petition: "Be not angry with the hunter, defend not thyself." The Lamutes of Siberia say: "Frighten us not, please. Die of thy own free will."

According to the Canadian anthropologist Marius Barbous the Bear myth is perhaps the most universal one among the Indians, because it includes all the elementary essentials: 1) the union between a supernatural being and a human being for the procreation of progeny who will share both the human and the supernatural attributes of the parents; 2) the agony to which the supernatural being voluntarily subjects himself to, for the good of the clan or of the entire community; 3) the ceremony derived from the myth in which those protected by the self- immolation of the supernatural being eat his sacred flesh as a special form of respect; 4) the function of intermediary between humanity and divinity that is assumed by the supernatural being.

Thus, the legend of the Bear-Martyr has elements that approach the life, the death, and the divinity of Jesus.

But I knew almost nothing about the Tlingit Indians who still live in Ketchikan, Alaska.

I answered: "There's an eagle on the top that must symbolize the emblem of the clan, the heraldic genealogy. Besides, there is the usual Raven seated atop the head of the Pisces Woman."

"That Raven," she said with a sigh, "is my father. And that woman is my mother."

Sighing, I asked: "And you carved your mother and your father for me? The colors are still fresh, my Princess."

"Don't you like them?"

"Of course, I like them! Very much!"

And with a shudder I immediately bethrought myself of my age: me, the Corvo of Salaparuta, her father; and Lisa, the Pisces Woman, her mother! An incestuous situation! But incest is as much abhorred among the Tlingit Indians as it is among Christians.

I learned later, by going through the findings of anthropologists Garfield and Forrest, that the Tlingit trace their descent through the maternal line, hence the crests of the totemic poles are not a family insignia but belong to the whole clan or to the line of genealogical descent. Every Tlingit belongs to one or the other of two subdivisions, or phratries, named after the Raven or the Wolf. Often the Wolves are called Eagles by some Tlingit tribes. All the Ravens are kindred and this also holds true of the Wolves (or Eagles).

Among these phratries there are smaller groups, or clans, whose members enjoy close bonds. The clans are subdivided into further groups or genealogical lines. Babies born into the group take on the mother's name, and, thus, they become not only members of her clan but also of the phratry. Since marriages between members of the same phratria are prohibited, the man and his bride always belong to opposite phratries: one or the other, accordingly, must descend either from the phratry of the Raven or from the phratry of the Wolf (or Eagle).

Among the Tlingit each genealogical branch owned hunting reserves, brooks, and bays where fish abound, houses and other properties. The houses were built of cedar wood so as to last a life-time, and they were large enough to accommodate several families. The hereditary chief presided over each house and administered the property and the affairs of each member. Personally, he was not the proprietor of the house — it was the common property of all the members of his lineage, including his mother and her brothers and sisters, and sons of his sisters. The children of his sisters lived with him, and upon his death, one of them would finally inherit his command, authority, and the responsibilities it entailed.

In the old days every Tlingit belonged to a hereditary class within which he was born and from which it was very difficult for him to escape. It was generally a class with an advantageous social tradition and one that was well-off economically. They also owned slaves, either captured during forays against neighboring peoples or bought from other slave-owners.

Later, Rose told me that her parents abandoned their smoked salmon factory in Ketchikan when, after the end of World War II, they began to lose money and business as a result of the installation of modern fish-drying plants and competition from foreign concerns. Their flight could not be to neighboring towns, it had to be definitive as a form of total forgetfulness. The

State of New York, through a competition of war veterans, seeded several acres of uncultivated land near the Mohawk River to her father for transformation into a dairy farm.

After the lengthy phone conversation, as pleasant as it was constructive, reverting to my usual irony, I said to her:

"You know, the Spirit is missing in class. Why don't you come back?"

"I don't understand why you call me by that name or the others as well."

"But you do understand the meaning of the figures on that totem, right?"

"It's the history of my family."

"Then you should also be able to understand Jung."

Rose did return to class. Now she looked like a real red Indian to me. She had accentuated her origins with her broad, red lips, and with her elongated eyes behind a veil of mascara and her smooth, almost oily, and self-cut raven black hair. Over her jeans she wore a white cotton T-shirt featuring the Ketchikan totem pole, painted in harsh and violent colors. The large blue wings of an eagle, or a falcon, atop the pole stood out protectively on her bosom.

"Would you like to explain it to the class?" I asked her.

"Must I really?" she smiled, looking uncertainly at her class-mates.

The students, twenty-five in all, immediately expressed their approval, urging her to take my place. Finally I sat in her seat and she sat in mine, looking as tall as the pole that identified her.

"As a premise," she began, "I would like to state that this totem is still situated in the exact place in which it was erected, between Mission and Stedman Streets in Ketchikan, Alaska. It belongs to the House of Kadjuk of the Raven Clan. It was carved and installed in its present location by the head of the clan, known as Chief Johnson, in 1901. My father, a member of the clan, was born in that year."

I shuddered. My father was also born in that year, but in Selimo, on the Adriatic Appennine Mountain Chain overlooking the beautiful and beloved Italian shores. And Rose herself was born in 1953, the same year in which my first book was published, which I called "son." While the real son, Sandro (the first of three), was born three years later. My father also had three children, as also did Rose's father.

I jotted down these notes. And she continued:

"Before Ketchikan was built, the members of the Kadjuk House and others from subordinated houses, owned the land at the source of the stream now called Ketchikan Creek. They had a summer encampment here and smoke houses where the salmon, caught on the spot, were laid out to dry for the winter."

She spoke slowly and tonelessly, as if she were reading from Garfield and Forrest.

"The legendary bird called Kadjuk can be seen at the top of the pole. It is as large as a blue falcon which it resembles, and it lives very high on the mountain, never descending to the lower peaks. Some say that its color is brown though the tips of its wings and of its tail are black, while others contend that the bird is white. It has not been seen for many years, but I believe that I once saw it when I was a child. The bird is the crest, or the emblem, of the administrative head of the Kadjuk House and nobody can use it without the Chief's express permission. Chief Johnson, who had the pole erected, was the administrative head of the Kadjuk

House in 1901, the year in which my father was born, a member of the same clan, namely that of the Raven."

Here she paused and emitted a prolonged sigh, after which she resumed her recital:

"The long smooth and undecorated space that separates Kadjuk from the other figures symbolizes the bird's elevated habitation and the great respect in which the crest, the heraldic sign, is held. The two bird figures, side by side, under Kadjuk are Gitsanuk and Gitsaqueq, slaves of the Raven who stands below them. The Raven's breast, as you can see . . . ," here Rose pointed to her stomach, "actually forms the hair-do of his wife below him, and his wings extend to both sides of her head. On her lower lip the woman is wearing one of the big plugs that indicate a woman of rank among the Tlingit people. In her hands she is holding two salmon, the first in the world, which she created. The two faces at the top of the tails of the salmon represent wealth in the form of two slaves carved higher up on the pole and, in addition, the wealth of fish that people now enjoy. She is called the Fog Woman. The Indians identify her with the in-between seasons when the fog hanging low over the source of the creek coincides with the mad salmon run to the sea. It was the Fog Woman," Rose concluded, "who created all the varieties of salmon, and put them in the streams."

"But do these figures suggest many stories or legends?" asked a student.

"No. All the figures on the pole, with the exception of Kadjuk, symbolize a unique story that stands out among the Raven's adventures."

"It would be of great interest to know the story," said another student.

"It's time to go," I interjected as I noticed students of another class impatiently pressing on the door to the lecture hall. As we filed out and walked towards the office I, unwittingly, grasped the hand of the girl who claimed to be the daughter of the Raven and of the Fog Woman.

8

Rose took the initiative to phone me a few days later. She wanted a book by Jung that had been recommended as supplementary reading for the course and that was not available in the library. I didn't have the car because Lisa had taken it for her trip to New Canaan. It was raining, and I had no desire to deliver the book by motorcycle. But since I didn't live far from the campus, she decided to brave the rain and come on foot.

I handed the book to her.

"But it's in German!"

Laughing, I intoned: "The Spirit manifests himself in all languages." Then I kissed her, and was kissed in return. Her lips were red and big, like plums. "The Spirit manifests himself in the form of a little flame. You have that flame in your mouth . . . "

She disengaged herself without really breaking away. We sat down on the rug, cross-legged, and the book fell between us. Carl G. Jung: *Symbolik des Geistes*.

"Why do you always pronounce that name? Even in class, it makes me feel ashamed. It strikes me as obscene."

"True," I murmured. "Obscenity is part and parcel of the sacred, my Princess."

"What have I got to do with that name?"

I picked up the book and opened it.

"You are called Spiram, and not Spearam. Nevertheless it's pronounced like spear."

"Like Shake-speare . . . ?" she laughed.

Since the encounter-seduction was becoming something like a lecture, and since it was raining outside, and since Lisa was away, I dropped Jung and picked up a dictionary, not without a twinge of self-consciousness in connection with the trick that I was about to play.

"Open it to the word *spir*, please."

She obeyed. "It's not here!"

"How about the word that follows?"

"The following word is *spirit*."

"Read it, please."

"Spirit: soul. God is pure spirit. We were with thee in spirit. Spirit of the time. Objective spirit. *Spiritus vegetativus*. The cold blasts of spirits. Are these phenomena really the work of spirits."

"And this is also your name," I observed. "*Spiram* means Spirit, and it must be the Christian translation of your Indian name. *Spiram* is the truncated form of *Spiramen* which in Latin means breath, but also means soul because the soul is essentially breath."

She lay the dictionary down, and I picked up Jung.

"Jung explains the matter more or less as follows. It's true that the breath is, in the first place, an activity of the body. But, viewed independently, it is a substance next to the body. If this concept is applied to the formula of the Trinity one quite properly could say Father, Son and *Life*, that is, Holy Spirit who proceeds from the Father and the Son, and is lived by both of them."

"Now you're losing me."

"The Father is the universal One, the Son is the *Other* of the Father, the Spirit is the Third in that he has emanated from both, that is to say he is common between Father and Son and points to an abolition of the duality."

"Why do you speak of duality between Father and Son?"

"Because both form an antithesis. The Father tries to maintain his being in oneness and loneness, while the Son strives to be another vis-à-vis the One. The Father does not want to release the Son because he would lose his character, and the Son detaches himself from the Father in order to exist. There is an antithetical tension between them. And as everyone knows, every tension of this kind drives towards an outlet, from which the Third derives, resolving the tension in the process. The Third is knowledge, vital breath. Jung says that the Triad is a development of the one in cognizability."

"Then you would be the Father . . . , " she murmured after a reflective pause.

Mentally recalling the totemic pole, I laughingly asserted: "In fact, they call me Raven . . . "

"Your wife would be the Daughter . . . "

"She is the Pisces Woman, in fact . . . "

"And I would be the Spirit breathed by the two of you . . . It's fantastic and obscene."

"My God, I'm not suggesting a *ménage à trois*. That would be terrible."

"Why terrible?"

I reached for one of Lisa's lipstick tubes lying in a nearby ashtray, picked up a sheet of paper in which I traced the scheme as drawn below:

PATER

FILIUS   DIABOLUS

"Because we would be reducing ourselves to this," I said, as I rushed to the brick cylinder. I stuck my head under the faucet and soaked myself like a pullet. My head was in a tangle, confused and bombarded from all sides. Nothing much was required, he mused, prattle about mystery and these girls literally fall into your arms. It was unsportsmanlike. It was to nobody's advantage to study the Trinity.

Upon emerging from the brick cylinder, brusquely, I said: "Let's go now, I'll take you back to the dorm."

The rain was still coming down hard, but they were wearing yellow raincoats and motorcycle helmets. They pierced the rain through the headlights of the motorcycle, an inebriating experience. The idea of sex and spirituality drowned in the anxious concern to avoid a fatal accident on the highway.

Of course, I continued to meet Rose by day or night, but secretly, and took her driving through the woods on my motorcycle. We made love on the haystacks and in roadside ditches. We ate in anonymous diners frequented by truck drivers. We joined other groups of motorcyclists. We bathed in the night in lakes under the moon, but Lisa's image often came between us, and in order not to chase it away (because they both love her) we resumed talking about the symbology of the One and of the Three.

Trine.

Triad.

Trinidad: an island in the Little Antilles.

Trinidad: a city in Cuba, on the Jayoba River.

Trinidad: a city in Uruguay, department of Flores.

Trinidad: a city in Colorado, U.S.A., on the Purgatoire River.

Trinity River: in Texas.

The Order of the Trinity: Medieval monks of love (1198).

Elsa Triolet: French woman writer.

Church of the Trinity: in Rome.

Bridge of the Holy Trinity: in Florence.

Trinitapoli: in Puglie, Italy.

Troy: a city in the State of New York.

Tri-City: Anabasis-New Wye-Eridanus.

Triolism: *ménage à trois*.

Troika: Russian carriage drawn by three horses.

Troilus: Priam's youngest son, killed by Achilles.

Terza Rima: see Dante.

Trinitrololuene: a high explosive.

I was assailed by terrible guilt complexes. I would have liked to break off the strange relationship with Rose. I now wished that nothing had come between us. Instead, she continued to sit beside me during my lectures.

One day Lisa and Judy passed by and stopped to peep in the window, their eyes went from me, who was talking to the class, to Rose, who was sitting beside me.

"She'll take him away from you," Judy murmured to Lisa.

Lisa reported Judy's warning to me who, irritated, replied: "So what if it should really turn out so?"

"If it should really turn out so, I'd be free!" she said, in a burst of laughter.

There was also the day when Lisa set out for New York, but she got a flat tire en route. She decided to return with the flattened tire and leave the job of changing it to me.

I was in the Pearls Gate with Rose. We both were at ease, drinking cola. And when Lisa suddenly appeared at the door Rose smiled at her. Instead, I hid my head under the pillow and tossed about like one obsessed.

"Spy, you did it deliberately!" I shouted.

Lisa ran off. She phoned Judy and Judy phoned Charlotte. Charlotte recommended that Lisa consult Susie Spring, the analyst, or Margie Lower, the divorce lawyer.

"A scandal of this kind can get Simon kicked out," Charlotte said.

"Simon can be kicked out only if they abolish his Department, an impossible task," observed Judy.

"We can bring that about, too. It's enough to want it to happen," threatened Charlotte.

Judy was now frightened, and told me about the conversation.

I telephoned Matthias, the Vice President, who had already been fully informed.

"I feel sorry for Lisa," he said.

"I'd like to punch a hole in Charlotte's belly."

"I'm handing in my resignation from this place next year," added Matthias. "There's altogether too much politics on the one hand, and altogether too much wordly-minded activity, on the other. We're all losing our tempers, all of us . . . Do you really want to stay on here?"

I knew that my days were numbered and cheered up. The scholastic year was coming to a close. I got on my knees and begged Lisa to forgive all my infidelities. Lisa pretended to believe me. She even invited Rose to dinner. We talked about the difference between sex and love, between *anima* and *animus* according to Jung, of the concept of the cave according to Plato, and of the concept of the three-legged horse according to Jung. Finally Lisa declared that she was madly in love with me, and Rose declared that she too loved me but not so madly.

"And whom do you love, Simon?" the two women asked.

"Charlotte!" I shouted in exasperation.

Several days later Rose Spiram left. She had been granted her degree. Her greatest aspiration was to become an airline stewardess, and even to obtain a pilot's license.

But soon after her departure, Lisa observed: "You're sad and sulky, love. Why don't you phone her? Why don't you invite her to spend a week-end with us?"

"A week-end? All three of us?"

"Why not? After all I like Rose and you like her, and we two ladies like you. Simple."

"Ridiculous. What do you want me to do with two women?"

"What do you know about what two women can do to you in the same bed?"

Finally it was Lisa who called her. Rose made some excuses. I picked up the phone to persuade her. She expressed the opinion that a separation was in the making between Lisa and myself, and she would not want to be its cause.

"No, not at all," I reassured her. "We merely want a threesome."

Rose finally arrived for a three-day stay. The triadic relation in fact lasted only three days, at the end of which an exasperated Lisa collapsed. She ordered Rose out of the house, and threatened to kill her if she ever showed up again.

Lisa was hysterical. She had many good reasons to be in such a state, and her only ideal now was to destroy my scaffolding one by one.

She, too, following Judy and Charlotte's advise, ended up visiting a shrink. The analyst was Susie Spring, Charlotte's secret bride. Lisa had become an extremely tenuous thread of nerves. Lisa had become a blinding streak of light. I truly loved her, but I knew very well that Lisa would leave me. In fact it was a matter of days, perhaps months.

And now seeing myself being turned out of doors, I invited little Satan G.O. and his wife, with ever greater frequency to my glass house.

G.O. had a soporific power over Lisa. He knew how to talk to her in a simple, vague kind of voice about his infinite solitude as husband, about his absolute lack of ambition and about his deep desire for a pure, disinterested loving relationship.

Lisa swallowed everything, and wildly recorded her physical and psychic experiences in her Diary. Often she left the notebook on the table of the brick cylinder open, so that I might read it. And I did. I also read about an afternoon when Susie Spring received Lisa in a nightgown, invited her into the bedroom where on the bed she saw Judy nude, smoking her fortieth cigarette of the day.

"Are we to repeat the threesome?" Lisa exclaimed, in mocking unbelief.

"There's an important difference," said Susie the analyst. "There are no men!"

Lisa, stunned, returned home. But she no longer protested, she sobbed for days on end, gripped me like a desperate woman, continually beseeching to be raped, to the point of total desperation, to the point of death itself.

"This is what death is," she murmured, "when life ceases to hurt."

9

The mail had been lying on the table since this morning, when Lisa left. I opened a letter from Italy and read:

> *Here we live waiting. Italy is knee-deep in scandals; the ruling class is more shameless than ever. Only the uninvolved save themselves, the obtuse. But, personally, I am very much concerned. After all it could also be described as a source of amusement and in reality I find it amusing. It's a farce Italian-style, with a pinch of Neapolitan pantomime. This entire establishment makes one laugh. Allow me to amuse myself, Palazzeschi used to say, and now I understand him, only it is not just a question of personal amusement. There is a fear of the aftermath, when the party is over. The party, in short, can be interrupted and transform itself into a tragedy. Terrorism has come upon the stage . . . And what are you doing in Anabasis, Nabokov County, Appalachia, U.S.A.?*

It was from Ugo, the gentlest homosexual I have ever encountered in the world. He lived in Rome as in a rose, wandering from a job in some ministry to one in the editorial room of some newspaper.

My mind roared.

What am I doing in Anabasis, Nabokov County, Appalachia, U.S.A.? I'm twiddling my thumbs, Ugo, as I'm doing on this very day, as my wife has left for New York City.

She took the Greyhound and got off at the Port Authority in New York around eleven in the morning. Then she walked down to Saks Fifth Avenue, slipped into the lady's room and saw her mother sitting there, reading *Cosmopolitan*.

Her mother took the train in New Canaan, she got off at the Grand Central in New York, walked down to Saks Fifth Avenue, slipped into the lady's room and saw her daughter sitting there, reading Joyce.

Whoever arrived first, waited.

They went to breakfast, they went shopping. Then the mother went to meet her lover whom she first met thirty-five years ago. He had children and grandchildren now, and over a vodka-martini they discussed business, fashions, and talked about remembrances. They no longer screwed, they were good friends. She bought him gold cuff-links each time she went on a vacation.

He was the one who replaced the Genovese officer whom she met during one of her vacations on the old stately liner Rex. She saw him regularly, thereafter, each time the Rex docked in New York. They loved each other passionately. Then the Rex no longer docked in New York, because it sunk during the World War II.

She became pregnant, although she had a husband in New Canaan, a French teacher. But she and her husband didn't love each other. It had been an arranged marriage, childless, and now she wanted a daughter from the Italian man.

The Italian died, and all that remained of him was this creature, Lisa, a daughter of the waves like Venus, thin-lipped and with a deep pubis.

She raised her like a marmot, very jealously, button by button, hat by hat. They slept together in the same bed, they wore the same dresses and when they were on vacation the fast-living baboons called them sisters.

It was in college that Lisa slept alone for the first time, and it was in the summer of 1960, in New York City, that she let a hunter possess her for the first time. And I was the hunter.

Lisa was either in Rizzoli's bookstore on Fifth Avenue or at a movie, waiting for the dinner hour with her mother, waiting to take the bus back to Anabasis. At times, like today, she slept in the city.

I remained alone at home, but I was not really alone.

When a union is based on trust, the risk of betrayal is a real possibility with which one has to live continually. Therefore it is part of the trust just as doubt is part of the living faith.

I remained alone at home, but I was not really alone. Since today was pay-day, the professorial paycheck went directly to the bank. I had no economic problem up to now unless my school went bankrupt, which was a probability, in which case I would have to end up as a jungle anthropologist for the Smithsonian Institute in Washington, D.C.. Or shoot myself.

Up to now no serious drama was in the immediate offing, except for a few little problems linked to my illness. Illness was useful when we realized that it is no longer possible to expel it.

Everything took another course. We slipped into the groove. And to register the fall signified to descend into the Avernus, among the Furies. But one adjusted even to this state of affairs.

See, what an optimist I am!

It's not true that only the sun and light are warming. Night was also tender. One can sleep. Indeed it's necessary to sleep for the morrow, for a moment or for a day that are still in the making. Hence I am alone but not really alone.

This nude glass house is vast and narrow. It seems to be made of furniture, objects. But when she's here it seems to be an extension of herself, and even time is no longer with me, she makes me act. But time is a vague cognition; the writer finds it by isolating himself, the lover by exhibiting himself, by talking, by caressing. The best time is always that spent with another person; the worst is with a blank sheet of paper staring at you and the memory that fills it. It is a time-frame as narrow and vast as this house.

Yet everything is going well and is still going well. I loaf about. I put on a record. I take a shot of gin. I go out to the meadow, then to the green house. The tomatoes are red and big on the stalks, as are the enormous rose-bushes in which one can mangle oneself. The squirrels scamper down from the trees and, like electric presences, they sniff about and run off. I go back to my study and look outside on the patch of woods. I feel her absence and desire her presence. I get drunk and get mixed up. The phone rings now and then, and finally all that remains is the blank sheet staring me in the face. I am a Xenophon, yes, trying to write my very private *Anabasis*. Remembrance is the only presence, along with sleep.

I sleep more than ever when she's not here, weariness accumulates and sleep shakes it off. I gently indulge in ironic self-reflection, observing my face in profile.

It's not true that I want to rid myself of my wife. But there is the illness, the physical illness, and the illness of the feelings.

What's the illness all about? Let's see.

Facial symptology. Symptoms: fierce pains in the ocular globe (internal), like stiletto thrusts. The eye contracts and closes. Sometimes it tears intensely. At other times, it is dry and sandy.

The nose begins to drip. A feeling of intense anxiety. A void in the stomach. Precipitate arrhythmia. Difficult breathing. A feeling of total depletion, as if all the blood has flown out (probably fall of pressure). At times, intestinal disturbances (diarrhea). The whole organism feels as though it's been shaken by a cyclone.

The crisis always occurs upon awakening in the morning. Sometimes it comes on during sleep and triggers the sudden awakening.

The first crisis occurred at the age of seventeen, when I was a prisoner of the Nazis in Villafranca, Verona. Diagnosed (badly) as neuralgia of the trigeminal nerve, it was never properly treated except with analgesics at the moment of crisis. In time the crisis increased in frequency and in intensity. They became intolerable during the marriage with Sibyl, the Roman wife. Doctor friends continued to talk about the trigeminal nerve, but some times the crisis occurred in the left eye, sometimes in the right eye, it always came from one side. Nobody had ever given that a thought!

Finally, a neurology professor made a correct diagnosis. His name was Shen, and he struck me as a character in James Joyce's *Dubliners*. He tried some treatments without results. The illness had now become chronic because too much time had passed and there was nothing more to be done: more than twenty years had gone by!

Relief could come only from a continual displacement from city to city or from continent to continent. The crises are provoked by meteorological phenomena, and by changes in the atmospheric pressure: storms, excessive heat, and excessive cold.

From the age of twenty to today (I am now forty-nine) I have dressed in the clothes of the unfortunate Leopardian Icelander, and have traveled throughout the world looking for the right climate, the right displacement. And this search had brought me to France, Lapland, Brazil, Amazonia, Egypt, Israel, Turkey, India, Labrador, on the Churchill Bay, California, Mexico, Morocco, Sicily, Senegal, Louisiana, the Caspian Sea (Kirkenes), British Columbia, Alaska, writing diaries and hefty anthropological works, shooting films, taking photographs, often surviving on bagels which I baked myself. I went to these places without knowing why I went there, nor why I wanted to go there. I wanted to feel better.

I lived all one summer in the woods in the Yukon, counting trees and fleeing from the blood-thirsty fury of the bears native to the region. I have crossed the United States from Seattle to Washington, D.C., in freight cars with drug addicts and pop musicians, recognizing and appeasing the criminal when he stuck a knife against my back. I have flown tin-plate planes, World War II rejects, in the storms of the Canadian arctic in order to retrieve frost-bitten geologists looking for uranium, and adventurers looking for traps belonging to others, and furred animals. They called me Jesus. And all this because I wanted to feel better. In the tundra women invited me to sleep on the white warmth of their thighs.

Yet, according to the neurologist Shen, the triggering cause of the crisis is certainly psychosomatic.

At the age of thirty-five I met Lisa Jones in a New York University classroom. I was now working in a kind of Arcadia called Accademia peopled by bilious men with red pencils and disarming smiles, and always in heat.

My eyes feel better now. I read, teach, and learn. And for several years, despite the difficulty of my relations with Lisa, the crises have almost disappeared. Relationship with Lisa had always been a capricious one, often because of her mother, who was hostile to thinkers. Lisa was also at fault because she missed Daniel, our son, who her mother, Cress, took away from us with the excuse that the child could not be subjected to our continual exploratory journeys to Tanzania, or on the Orinoco, during which we often ate white worms for breakfast.

As a result of the deterioration of the relation with Lisa, the crises have reappeared of late, increasing in frequency and intensity. I have become Job. Most of the time the crises were resolved by keeping the eyes closed and contracted, almost strabic. The eyes then open and normalize with the passage of time.

My ophthalmologist in Anabasis, Big Peter, diagnosed it as glaucoma, a veritable social illness because of its frequency (it affects more than 2 percent of the world population over forty), which is characterized by an increase of ocular pressure which determines a gradual loss of sight. I learned that Milton became blind as a consequence of glaucoma, and the same was true of Homer. I am neither Milton nor the blind Homer, to be sure, but only a man frightened of the darkness.

At the present time, however, the crises were only rarely very acute. I continue to treat them with analgesic's (two tablettes of Nisidina) the moment they start. Then I stay in bed and try to read. During an acute crises I get some relief by eating bagels usually, or chewing even bits of cement plastering which I scratch off the walls of a nearby ruined farm building.

A violent quarrel can also serve as a safety valve, and make me feel better.

What am I doing in Anabasis, Nabokov County, Appalachia, U.S.A.?

I'm twiddling my thumbs. I'm doing this on the very day that my wife has left for New York.

Not true! I'm taking a stroll on my wife's love diaries.

10

A brief, glorious pre-puberty nursery age, the best moment spent together with another body, as small as mine, ambitious, indefatigable, a big and generous smile.

The exploration of unknown cavities, the splits that gave no account of themselves. "Let me look at it again!"

Each discovery that had to be classified was excitedly divulged on the handle bars of bicycles, at first in whispers, slowly growing into shouts of joy. This was followed by a very fast race around the walls of the school and then by a return visit to the old garage for the confirmation.

Erotic symptoms?

Certainly.

But there was something vital and delicious in what we were doing.

❑

In that old and moldy garage covered with ash and its dusty windows, small and trustful worlds little by little became more intense, intimate. Two private suns. Someone might be spying. But no such thing happened. A descent of paranoia on our shoulders. Anxiety. Then a call from the nearby house. The instant dissolution of the enchantment.

"Pull up your pants!"

A belt being buckled, one of the things of secret hours.

There was certainly envy, but that did not exclude delight.

To piss in a bottle.

A mother, a man. He was fat and did not seem to be my father. We called him Prick. A father who smiled when I looked at him.

Lamentations of cats in Spring. Lacerating lamentations that could make you faint. Then the hormones. We ran with the first rackets. Bursts of laughter.

One hot summer night somebody called me into a tent. Dark confusion, I ran away. And if he had raped me?

❑

Baseball, roller skates, arid desert of people. Pure air. A marvelous, virile, smiling man appeared, full of knowledge, and with eyes that sparkled.

Officially the principal of a high school, and I observed for four intense years, and I blushed, and thoughts flowered. Adrenaline flowed. And finally it focused as man.

The thoughts remained inside me, only music went in and out. Coltrane, Parker, Evans. They said love and had my love. Once again different hours at the violin, prolonging the sounds that only I heard, until a rainy day arrived, the sofa was soft, oh how I would let myself be taken now, the rain, the sofa, and nobody came, yes, nobody came, spring rain. How old must he be now? Thirty-five, forty?

Warm is the color of two, side by side.

❏

Projection, desire, then something else sprouted. And I dived into it, each time it was an eddy, and I always asked for more.

"You almost have no hair on your head."

All the hair was on the strong thorax, and all the will was in that hooked nose of his.

Then I dreamed little of him, except for certain nightmares in which I was Lady Macbeth.

It was a misfortune that the breasts were so small that they could not be contained in a bra.

But the eagle will spread her wings. Poor deluded girl! Fear of the gossip of the little city. Race towards the big city.

It was difficult to eye young men after what had happened. Because they could not and would not do what I would have liked.

❏

Today we made love in the afternoon. It is Tuesday, April 24, 19 . . .

It was on a Tuesday afternoon that I came upon them together, him and Rose. The memory of the scene is so alive that today, while we were making love, I got to thinking that he was comparing me to her.

We made love in the small glass room area that he calls the Pearls Gate, on the battered mattress which we had used during the first years of our marriage. It had become flaccid and lumpy with the passage of time.

No matter how much I beat it in the meadow and spray it with special detergents, it still smells, and the effect is suffocating. It's like dried-out leather and horse manure in stables.

I passed my tongue over it. Especially during the afternoons of dizziness, when he was away at school. I licked the dry roses of sperm which today are rusty like decalcomanias, and thus gave vent to my venery.

Today, it no longer attracts me.

He bought it at a sale in Scarsdale, Westchester County, N.Y., when Cress, my mother, bought us our first house in 19 . . . I didn't sleep much in it because, at that time, I was pregnant with Daniel and I spent a great deal of my time in New Canaan where my mother insisted I should give birth.

Daniel's birth coincided with Simon's first clamorous break with my mother. Cress evicted him from that house.

She insisted that I should divorce him, reminding me that she had two savings bank books for me: the first, containing a modest sum, was for my studies; the second, containing lots of money ($395,000!), was for my adulthood — when I would have found the man that she, too, would have approved as a groom, that is to say when she would have made the choice for me.

Since I had made an insane choice by marrying Simon, she now wanted me to divorce him. She adduced two reasons: 1) she was afraid of Simon's intelligence and independence, considered as important as her own intelligence and independence; 2) I and the baby, by living with her in the same house, would serve as a shield against the flaccid presence of her husband, whose wretched existence had been reduced to correcting homework assignments in elementary French, and to walking our dog in the garden.

She had never taught me to call him *Dad*.

Like everybody else, in fact, I called him Prick: a diminutive for Patrick? And he said nothing, never a word. He was totally aware of and offended by his situation, but he could not escape, nor had he ever wanted to escape. I believe that Cress, jealous and displeased, must have been wrecked for many nights and days by the crazy notion that the stranger Simon was none other than her Italian lover who had died at sea at the outbreak of World War II. And that now, transformed, he had come back to her in the guise of Simon in order to retrieve his daughter by marrying her and relegating Cress to unsmiling old age and withered widowhood.

Desperate, my mother had even attempted to have him arrested in connection with the disappearance of some jewelry from the house in New Canaan, one Sunday, when Simon had remained alone at home, while we had gone to a wedding.

Simon told the police that he had been on the porch, reading. And he declared that he had never set foot in the house, not even to fetch himself a glass of water. My mother had hidden the jewels in some drawer, but I didn't believe that she had done so purposely. In fact, she found them years later when, to her resigned eyes, Simon and I began to appear as a well-matched, compatible couple.

When she evicted him from Scarsdale, Simon realized that he had his back to the wall. He had always said that the world was against him. But he did not want to be saved. He did not want to end up like Prick, the man who would have been so happy if I had called him "Pa." Simon sold everything he had bought for our house, keeping only his books and his mattress. He rented a U-Haul and dragged that mattress back to his old studio in New York City, on East 94th Street.

I didn't want to divorce him but, in this situation, it was not even possible to live together. The hemorrhages that afflicted me after the baby's birth were of great help to my mother in her plan to super-protect me, and keep me for herself.

I had already recovered. I wanted and desired him so I went to New York once a week — even though Cress's approval contained a tacit reproach — and I became his week-end prostitute.

I carefully checked that mattress for signs of other occupants, but all I could detect was the cat's hair. But I could not reproach him; because he waited for me and I for him.

I really wanted to stay with him and start all over again. I urged him to take me away as quickly as possible because I, too, wanted to escape from my mother's overbearingness. He understood my plea and made a further sacrifice. He gave up his teaching career at NYU and accepted a teaching job in Vancouver, Canada, which paid less but the university had a fine supply of monkeys.

And I didn't even know where Vancouver was!

"It is located on the northern Pacific Coast. It is beautiful, hygienic. Our son will grow up there and become a fisherman," he said.

That was fine. But I had already decided to leave Daniel with my mother. I had no desire to play the mother role. Besides, my mother was only too pleased to learn how to be a grandmother. But Simon insisted that I should return to fetch him once we were settled down. I agreed and we started to load all our belongings and put the mattress, of course, on the '63

Imperial, the automobile which my mother had given us as a gift.

From the East we set out for the Northwest, using the mattress in the orchards, and on the edge of roads in the South, on the beaches of California, and in the woods of Oregon. When we stopped he would pull that mattress out of the car. And once on the ground the mattress became home.

We called the mattress Byron and Milly Bloom, Molly's Daughter. He was Byron; I Milly.

One morning, as we were making love on the mattress in our new Vancouver house, we were paralyzed with fear by an earthquake tremor. Crouched, he remained inside me when the TV set fell from the stool amid the blowing noise of shattered window panes.

Shuddering he said, "I've impaled you, I can't pull it out!"

I panicked and forgot all about the earthquake. I had read about cases of priapism in medical pocket books, about how they required medical intervention. To have the doctor or the ambulance take us to the hospital fastened to each other was the last thing I wanted. On the other hand, I wanted to get out of the house.

Luckily it was a lightquake. He said: "You'll see, there'll be no further quakes. We should phone First Aid, though!"

When he lifted me up I realized that I was soaking wet. It was blood. I figured that my menstrual period had begun one week in advance of schedule perhaps provoked by my fear. I was dripping all over his legs as he carried me across the room and down the stairs to the kitchen where the phone was located. We lived in a two-storey house on the edge of the campus.

"There's only one way to do it," he said, laughing. "Origen's cut!"

Upon finally reaching the room below, Simon freed himself with a sudden backward thrust. He set me down on the couch.

In between nervous outbursts of laughter and weeping, I began to lick the blood off his legs.

"Why did you want to scare me?"

"So as to make you forget the real scare, the earthquake."

I had already forgotten everything. The scattered pieces of the TV set were all that remained of the earthquake's arrival. And the puddle of blood on the mattress was all that remained of Simon's priapism.

He gathered up the splinters of glass, while I washed the mattress with a duster. And then while I was cleaning up the mess, desire seized me again. Unfinished business tugged inside me like anxiety.

The fucking lasted all day. This time it was different from any other time because we felt like people who had miraculously escaped disaster.

On the following day, he paid homage to me by presenting me with one of his poems — a rare courtesy. It was titled *New Life*. I didn't understand its meaning, except for the allusion made to the blood on the stairs.

I wanted to free myself of the mattress. I wanted a king-size bed, but Simon pretended he did not hear me. For awhile I did not insist. I knew that he was fond of that mattress because it symbolized familihood. To part with mattress would have signified the break-up of the home. Like wife-swapping. Traditional Italians like him, stemming from immigrated peasants, change mattress only when one of the spouses dies. Divorce and carnal separation are like death for them.

His face contorted when I told him that I was fed up with life in Vancouver and that he should find a new job in the States.

"America is where I am," he said.

Later he accepted a position at the University of California. We transferred ourselves to Oakland with the mattress duly loaded on our '63 Imperial.

We set up our home in Berkeley on Keeler Avenue. We had flowers and fountains and a swimming pool. Daniel continued to remain with his grandmother in New Canaan. I felt no particular affection for him, though he became a consolation for my mother. Poor woman. Simon protested, but I told him clearly: "If you insist, you will have neither me nor Daniel. I'll divorce you."

The statement was a slap in his face. He finally gave in to my threat. We made many trips together yet he would avoid going to New Canaan to meet his son, except for one time when he took Daniel to visit Philip Johnson's *Glass House*.

When, in 1967, I told him that I was also fed up with California and that I wanted to return to New York City, he almost hit me.

"According to you," he said, "am I to start all over again from scratch? Leave a job to find another just as I'm getting acclimatized to it?"

He stormed out of the house and went fishing on the Grand River in the Rocky Mountains. When he came back, he was in a totally different state of mind. He said that he had met a doctor and a chemist from Anabasis, Appalachia, and that they had suggested that he transfer and go to work with them.

This move turned out to be easy. In Anabasis he designed and built in four months a glass house modeled after Philip Johnson's *Glass House* in New Canaan which he greatly admired. "It might also be a Dosto-evskian *glass house*, who knows?" I did not know, but we finally bought, at long last, a king-sized bed.

The old mattress now found its proper place in a small glass room. I had the presentiment that this transfer would bring about not only a slight alienation from the mattress but from ourselves as well.

When Simon's off-campus colleagues came for lectures, they slept on that mattress in the small glass room. When Daniel came from New Canaan, he slept on the mattress. When his sons came from Italy or when his friends from all countries came for a visit they slept on that mattress.

One day Simon invited Rose to lie on the mattress. And today, Tuesday afternoon, he brought me there.

11

We have made love in the afternoon so many times. We did not have daily office hours. A professor is always free, even when he is working in the office or at home. Sex is the logical sublimation of this work.

Today's American academic life encourages non-stop production and little specialized work which requires years of research. There is no longer a need for the masterpiece from the historian, the philosopher, or the man of letters. No need of great books. Rather, it demands quickly put together textbooks.

Aware of this monotonous regularity, Simon produces studies and monographs whose quality he is not content with. But these works permit him to remain on the uppermost rung of the ladder.

University publications and research studies have only the frame of past humanistic passion. Today we publish only to attain political positions within the administration, or to be promoted and to obtain lifetime tenure.

Given the economic restrictions that weigh on private and state universities alike, and to avoid dismembering of departments by firings which lead to court suits and litigation that last for years, department heads must often turn to private foundations for donations. This is how programs are kept alive.

Simon is almost always involved in campaigns for the collection of hundreds of thousands of dollars so as to assure the livelihood of his monkeys and of his experiments. He not only immerse himself in conferences and embark on trips of all kinds but also produces, with Andrew, scientific spectacles that show how sex should be taught in schools at all levels since sex lies at the base of every human and social activity.

When he comes back home from the laboratory or seminars, he often invites friends and students home. They talk, write, study labyrinthine maps, or just listen to music. One never leaves the classroom with Simon. He writes, paints, plays the organ, rides a motorcycle, works in the garden, cooks, visits his monkeys. He dapples on everything, but above all he is a consummate conversationalist. In his gloomy moments, he repeats: "I was born dead. I belong to the times of Leon Battista Alberti. Those times have gone forever!"

The parties we give, Simon does not deduct from his income tax as professional expenses, despite my insistence to do so. Though those gatherings involve cultural activities linked to his professional work, he prefers to deduct only his trips rather than exploit his social encounters and friendships.

We have many friends but Cara and Bart, Peter and Punks are the ones closest to us. Rare are visits from Matthias and his wife, Sue. Nevertheless we enjoy a perfect harmony with them. We are not in agreement on everything with Simon; we instinctively realize that each one of us would have done exactly what he or she planned to do, sharing the woe or the weal ensuing from an action. But in the matters of love we have always been in agreement and, like Simon, I prefer love in the afternoon, those siesta hours in which I melt away and swoon.

During spring I change my panties twice a day, and don't wear any at all in the summertime. Often in spring, desire suddenly comes over me while I'm in the car or in the library or watching the bulge in the pants of someone walking alongside me. I never raise my eyes when I walk, but I do keep them half-raised. I check the point of my sandals and that which appears to me at medium level, that is, legs and bodies. I then check the face and body trunk, the legs and, again, I lower my eyes and stop on the point of my sandals. At home, however, I complain if Simon is not there. I vent my feelings by getting down to work on my Ph.D. thesis which, given the state the market is in, is worth nothing.

Recently, I have not made love in the afternoon for several weeks. And it is for this reason that I suspect Simon of having compared me to Rose.

The little three-quarter bed, the mattress of our first years of marriage and now of his affair with Rose, was a premeditated choice on his part.

"This is the bed of sex," he told me once," whereas the other, the king-size, is the bed of love."

I understood what he meant, but now I also know that I am very jealous of that mattress in the small glass room. Is love jealous? I considered myself as having been brought up in a system that views jealousy as a crime against the independent person. I was mistaken. Jealousy gnaws away at me and, at times, makes me see things through dark, tragic, movie-like tones. I see everything around me crumbling, and I'm afraid of dying under the ruins.

While he was caressing me, I was thinking of Rose, then of Rose with us two, she in my skin and in his, I with her and with him; and she with me and with him. I became so ecstatic over these thoughts that, as a result of persistently pursuing them further, I began to suddenly swoon.

My whole body was suffused by a supreme, sinking feeling of utter sweetness. A Van Goghian sun appeared before my eyes, one which I had seen the first time as an adolescent, while I was dreaming of love. The sun was in my eyes and face; I saw myself as being tattooed with sunflowers. But soon the mind resumed its dominion over the senses and the torturing ceased. Has Rose ever enjoyed a moment like this? Has she ever taken a shower together with him?

I was now sexually passive. Rose was not with us and now I was with her, even if for a certain period of time I had not given myself to Simon but to Rose. But my pleasure was followed by the anxiety that he may love her more than me, and this gave the afternoon a touch of sadness. My thoughts were inconsistent for, after all, Simon did love me well and very effectively.

Forgetfulness was devastating until he brought it to a conclusion in an absolutely new way: He withdrew from me. This was exceedingly strange since I was taking my pill.

"Why did you do that?" I asked him, flabbergasted.

I felt unwell. Now I was certain that he had been thinking about Rose while making love to me. But he quickly drew me to himself again, adjusted his body to mine.

He said, "Let's sleep now. It was very beautiful!"

He slept like a baby, sucking a nipple while I caressed his hair. I didn't know if I loved him. He had given me comfort, he had given me pleasure. I asked, "Has Rose ever had something like this?"

"Why do you bring her up for?"

"I would have liked her to have been with us this afternoon."

"It's a thing of the past, over and done with. Does it still bother you?"

"Not anymore. But I would like to be her friend."

"Are you looking for trouble?" he said.

I took his hand and placed it on my breast. I wanted to be adored. Which he understood. His kisses gave me the unexpected urge to eat cheese. And in fact we did eat some cheese together, in a big hurry, soon realizing that we both had to go back to work. As we were getting into the car I became extremely curious and asked: "What kind of orgasms does Rose have?"

He did not answer. He looked sad.

We parted company in the parking lot, he walking toward his office, I toward the library. It felt like a real separation. We even forgot to make the customary appointment to meet later so that we could go back home in the only car we had. This had happened before but we always ended up waiting for each other in the parking lot.

Determined to continue my work on the *Dubliners*, I went to my cubicle in the library. But a message scotch-taped on the door made me change my mind. "If you'd like a coffee, you'll find me at Cunaxa's." It was from Slingerlink, an affable Renaissance scholar.

I went to the bar, which professors called Cunaxa. Simon called it *cuna*, Italian for cradle. When he would sometimes get drunk over there he used to call it *defeat*.

Matthias and Zinghelli were having a martini with Slingerlink. They looked at me and guessed that I had just been making love. I did not care. I shut my eyes and again felt normal.

12

You come to look for me in the library to my utter surprise. You smile at me and rest your hand on mine caressingly. I find that very strange, you know.

What remains is not this particular minute but yesterday afternoon. The night following the afternoon spent together in the usual room and in the usual bed had been so canceled out that you now beside me cannot help me recall the many other nights of our life spent together. I'm in a state of remorse or weariness. If you were to ask me, as you always do, to write down what we did last night or what we ate, the phone calls received, I would not be able to write anything down. I don't remember a thing about last night. And now you come and you ask me with your strange smile: "Are you feeling better?"

When you notice my diary open on the table, I understand your curiosity. Without the slightest hesitation I say, "You can read it, if you wish."

But as I am telling you to read it, I realize that you have already done so. I see you flip through the pages, thanks to your speed-reading skills, at a rate of 500 words per minute. This horrifies me.

Usually you read a book in a half hour, and annotate it in two hours after a re-reading. You read 30/40 books a week while it takes me three days to read a novel, five for a James novel. I can spend two weeks in re-reading it and making notes.

What amazes and horrifies me is your racing around in a thousand and one directions. It disorients me, leaves me behind.

You say: "I've the impression that you have invented 90% of your feelings by committing them to writing, and now that they are down on paper they serve as an alibi every time for when you feel like accusing me of something."

"Writing's my way of establishing my point of view of a certain situation," I retort.

Then you pick up the diary and say, "I'll now write my point of view right above this, O.K.?"

You go out and come back fifteen minutes after. "It's all here. Now I'm going back to my office. As for tonight . . . if you'd like, come pick me up and we'll go home together."

I pay no attention to what he says. I begin to read what he has written:

> It began this way, Lisa, a few minutes ago in your cubicle where, full of love, I dropped by for a visit. You wanted to ask me why I had a strange smile on my face, but you did not do so. You sat back in your seat in order the better to determine whether a relationship between you and me still existed. Your diary is more intelligent than accurate, and now you are using it to erect walls. Instead of making revelations in the diary you begin to hide things and to hide yourself. The diary of your life in New England, that I asked you to write at the be ginning of our relationship in New York, had a greater "purity."

That I compare you? I didn't even remember that yesterday was Tuesday. Last Tuesday, the one you speak with Rose, had been canceled from my memory. I simply don't understand why you should insist upon bringing it up. Actually, I know why: Tuesday serves your purposes more than mine. This is so because you want to run away. You are at a crossroad and are looking for a big excuse to run away. I compare you?

Rose wasn't at all on my mind yesterday afternoon when I was making love with you. And yesterday, as many, many times before, it was beautiful to make love to you. Would you like to know what two professors of mathematics were saying today as they were eating their sandwiches prepared for them by their wives the night before? "Do you do it regularly?" They confessed to each other that it was no longer regular, perhaps once a month. And one of them admitted with an appalling metaphor, "We are like two blocks of marble in the graveyard of our bed."

Oh, Lisa, if our love dies it will not be because of Rose. It's convenient to play the injured party. The difficult thing is learning, if we want to continue to be together, and re-discovering ourselves with absolute probity. Shall we try it?

I close these notes and feel hollow inside. Try? I would like to, but I am more disenchanted than ever. One gets used to love the same way one gets used to suffering. Why not try it?

The sufferance of love is some thing that could be overcome by other commitments, indeed by other loves. But what I don't want now is to be left alone with myself. I want to be "me," and no longer me with "you" or in terms of you.

Father Confessor, my confessions began from the moment that you asked me to confess so that you could nourish yourself on me. Now I'm going to throw every thing topsy-turvy. All alone I shall set for that great experience. At age thirty-three, all that beckons me is precisely that great experience. And at this point I avail myself of your beloved Jung: "The *One* does not wish to choose the *Other* because he is afraid of losing his character, and the *Other* breaks off from the *One* in order to exist."

I am the *Other,* Simon.

(And, besides, I hate this clever city made up only of Homer Parkways, Aristophanis Lanes, Cyrus Street, Lysander Squares, Georgias Avenues, Leontini Roads, Agamemnon Alleys, Myron Crossroads, Sparta Super-markets, Plato Shoemakers, Hesiod Laundromats, Sappho Cookies, Demeter Restaurants, Orphic Taverns, Delphis Aerobic Health-Spas.)

13

Another crisis . . .

Now all the lies with which we have lived no longer function. Lies and illusions are intercommunicable. Being one and the same thing, they are necessary for one who advances in life with an appearance of well-being. But when we see the light, life appears to us as boredom and mental distress. Such a life lacks permanence.

Often I find myself thinking about man during the Middle Ages. He knew little more than fear, sickness and death. Yet he was ensconced in the comforting faith that the universe had a purpose because it had been created by God's sapient hand. And even though this man was nothing else but a grain of dust in nature, he was still part of the design of God who was absolute and permanent.

We all need permanence. This, too, signifies an ignorance of the nature of things. At the base of today's experience there is the agonizing awareness that everything is unstable, everything is flux, words, lies.

I know very well that we create these lies for ourselves in order to preserve our attachment to the illusion of permanence. The lie is the capital of storekeeperism. Only it's different for me now. I had attached myself so firmly to our reciprocal lie of permanence in love that now that it has surfaced I am upset and feel lost. I'm a fish out of water gasping for breath. I needed this illusion. I always wanted something to which to attach myself. I'm a believer. And what I have always wanted, in order to sustain myself in life, is what Rose and you have taken away from me.

I've once thought of committing suicide. Do you think it's something to laugh about? This time it was in order to punish myself for what I have seen. I don't want to tear my eyes out only because these eyes have seen. I want to tear myself radically away from you, Simon, from the life that you represent for me.

This idea of suicide is subtle and perfidious. It is so absolute that it resembles certain of our afternoon sessions, when I felt as though I couldn't breathe, when I felt as though I was about dying, suffocating under abundance. It usually happens to me when I ask you for what is forbidden. You tie my wrists behind my back with a nylon string from your guitar and you blindfold me with one of your colored kerchiefs. It is I who wants to be tied, it is I who wants to be gagged. I admit it, so don't protest. For this is my game of love and death, even if you satisfy it reluctantly, thinking I'm a sick chick.

Well, I am sick. But this is how I've discovered the peak pleasure of coming. And once this fantasy is removed, the other idea crops up: to slash the veins on my wrists and then let them be sewed up in time, before boredom supervenes.

The first time this idea occurred to me was when we were lovers in Manhattan. I believed that I had lost you because you had gone back home, probably to reconcile with your wife: this idea has never been totally erased in my mind. Your wife remains dozing and almost lost in the folds of my mind. She beats like a heart, at times she rises like a wing and I observe her, timid and bewildered at the beginning. She is small and bloodless as I watch over her. I breathe under her living shadow, a black wing darkening everything around it.

She usually appears to me in the evening when I think of you being with Rose, after you have given your last class. A wing whirls around my head, whirling around the peak point of my fragility, becoming a whirlwind, and finally a mirage. She is like Virginia Woolf in her white dress walking into the waters of the river. A mirage, and then, in a flash she is no more. Little bubbles linger at the point where she has stopped walking. The river has not left its course for a moment. One evening I survived and when you returned I say, "Don't you think, Simon, that suicide is the sincerest form of self-criticism?"

You laughed, most embarrassedly.

In the last few days you have been working on an essay on Pavese, welded together around the theme of suicide. The books you used as bibliographical sources are still around the house: Durkheim, Frazer, A. Alvarez, Morselli, Wittgenstein and Anne Sexton. And in a footnote to your *curriculum vitae* you have written that you yourself, at the age of seventeen, had attempted to commit suicide. You wanted to kill yourself because you had been disappointed by something.

You laughed, embarrassed. You managed to assume a swaggering tone, and replied, "As we grow older, becoming gnomish, suicide strikes us as ever more improbable because there's so much less to kill."

"But you're driving me to suicide," I answered.

"No, no. You're a coward. You'll never make another attempt to do away with yourself."

"I've never tried."

"Have you forgotten April 18, 1962?"

"It was a farse."

"In a telephone booth next to the New York Public Library. Have you forgotten?"

"I said it was a farce."

"I always knew that. You wanted me to feel sorry for you. You delicately cut your wrists with my razor. Then you phoned me and asked me to rush you to the hospital. There, with your wrists in bandages, the moment I entered your room, you said, 'I want to make love.' And then I went to Mexico to get my divorce, and later, in our state of euphoria, we conceived a child in Provincetown, Cape Cod. Then we had ourselves married by a Justice of the Peace, by trade a mechanic, in Vermont, not telling a soul about it. Your attempted suicide at the time, precisely because it was a farce, has brought us to these outrageous days . . . "

"I was afraid that you'd leave me . . . "

"I should have done so!"

"I was silly . . . "

"You mean that now it's serious?"

"It's different now, because we're different."

"And you want to commit suicide because we are different?"

"I'm taking formal note of the end of the lie."

Both of us were in a pathetic state. You bent over to kiss me, Simon, but we were also laughing like a tubercular patient spitting blood. For a moment I thought that you were the real suicide. Instead you merely wanted to play around again and get me back.

Pages of my thesis were stained with whiskey and tears, and were spread out on the rug. Looking at them, you said maliciously, "No, my dear. Suicides are a thing of the past. Once they were the aristocrats of death, God's neo-graduates. Instead of writing their thesis, they wanted to impersonate them, thus proving how limited the alternatives that God has granted to himself and to his creatures are. The show they put on became magnificent literary criticism: Hart Crane, Randal Jarrell, Hemingway, Mark Rothko, Cesare Pavese, Yukio Mishima. These were people who still wanted to offer something. But by growing older, suicide fails. There's nothing more to kill. And you are old, Lisa, and a coward."

You went into the kitchen to make yourself a tunafish sandwich. You were whistling. I got up, made my way to the garage quietly, started the car, pulled out of the driveway, and drove along the highway at a crazy speed, hoping for an accident.

You see, Simon, after I came upon you with Rose, you rebelled against my reactions of rage and real pain. You accused me of treating you like a piece of property. You told me that you were my bank account, my fur coat, my house, my studies, my friends. The false sense of stability comes to me from the fact of having a husband or a house or a bank account, which is your bank account. The sense of instability comes to me from you because my trust consists in my being attached to you.

I brokedown with the end of my only true illusion: the lie that somehow you guaranteed me stability and a certain permanence in my life. I trusted our love was different from my past loves and your loves that had preceded ours. I believed that your love would be permanent. Now I realize that all unions are condemned, mine and yours, as well as Rose's with you. In our stupid search for a long-lasting union, we have suddenly ended up alone.

It's not only a matter of loneliness. Our sacred lie is no more, that lie which, often, wreathes absolute loneliness with a smile.

I shall have to learn the harsh lesson of living without a lie, of living in the present without further need for drugs or karma. Once trust is no more all that remains is the naked reality. Disconsolate, upset, we move and live our being like two strangers.

I have loved you, Simon: a fantastic elf, an elderly seducer who suffused me with animation. Now the animation has flown away, and I've become a rag.

14

How did the new crisis arise?

One night Simon was dining out with members of the faculty and a candidate for the position of Assistant Professor in his department.

For the last few weeks there had been interviews, conferences, and also many dinners. Charlotte felt outraged by the male world. From her observation post in the Inner Circle she persistently pointed out to various deans and vice-presidents how necessary it was to re-evaluate the position and the status of women in civil service jobs, particularly when they are academics.

Both she and Matthias insisted on publications, research and teaching in the classroom as a basic qualification prior to any appointments and promotions. Although men were not much better prepared than women, reality indicated that they had more experience, including job experience, behind them. Though they were excellent researchers, women continued to receive unfavorable reports from their male colleagues, either because their publications were scarce or of a quality inferior to those of male aspirants.

Charlotte herself had published very little and, in the opinion of male judges, what was published was second rate. A memorandum to the President, signed by a group of males with alleged high qualifications, stated that Charlotte's "publications are, in our view, below the academic standard." Charlotte, notwithstanding, undaunted, held her head higher than ever, perhaps ignorant of the stake at which she would be burnt alive one day.

Simon had mixed feelings in regard to her. He admired her yet felt sorry for her. At times, when he was enraged, he called her a plagiarist.

That night it was again a matter of bringing a male to dinner. I had been invited, but I refused, taking Charlotte's side. I, too, began to be annoyed by these bronzed and virile males, bearded, with the science of lofty scorn in their words and in their idol-like movements.

Oh, Simon! You tried to estrange me during this winter of discontent. True, you were working very hard at all hours and, in addition, you had to cope with some troubles that had arisen in your department. You were frustrated, deprived of the normal passage of day and night, you ate badly, your eyes hurt, your stomach hurts, and for some strange reason you wanted to be alone to meditate. I knew that you were unhappy with our life.

You often said that you couldn't take the regularity with which our life proceeded: we were always together, you complained at home, in the bathroom, in school, at the movies, in the supermarket.

I would reply: "It's because of the cold, it will pass."

Yet that cold had paralyzed our emotions. I refused your invitation to dinner in order to leave you free, so I accepted an invitation to go to the movies with Judy and her new friend from the philosophy department, Allen Murdock. I shouldn't have done it, because you detested Judy. She knew too much about our affairs. And Judy, in fact, does know everything.

She is the friend to whom I turned on the evening of that terrible Tuesday when I discovered the both of you at home in the small glass room. After the recriminations, the shock and the sense of loss occasioned by that encounter, you brought Rose, who herself was in a state of shock and bewilderment, back to the dormitory. You say, "Don't wait for me. I've got some people to see."

By that you meant to say that you'd be back later or, perhaps, that you wouldn't come back at all. That night I wanted you to come back no matter what and only for the purpose of continuing the clash we had in the afternoon. I had a great advantage over you, and I wanted to exploit it. You're a salamander, you cover yourself with ashes when you're in the fire.

My fragility lies in my inability to be alone.

The glass house appeared like a trap to me. I bit my hands, my eyes were puffed. I phoned Judy and she came immediately, concerned, affectionate, to take me to her apartment on Cyrus Street, where she plied me with Scotch and supportive attention.

"So Lisa, you've been through it, too."

She sat down next to me on the sofa, ready to listen to everything, even though she already knew everything.

Judy was now living her exclusive moment, free of Punks' surveillance, like a spider in possession of the whole web.

I let myself be pitied, half drunk as I was with Scotch and tears, her hands in mine, like two sisters, I empathized with her nakedness, and she with mine.

She advised me to see Susie Spring. I suddenly felt ashamed of myself: I was becoming your enemy. Even if I had not gone to see her personally, Judy would have attended to this matter on her own and Susie, in turn, would have informed Charlotte, and Charlotte, Matthias. Soon the Cyrus Street world would be embracing a new sister and a divorce to boot. Revenge would be mine.

Again, I was deeply ashamed of myself. Shame is nothing when it alleviates an offense. Judy, however, was understanding and tactful, and you hated her for this. She had become a shield between us. This is why when she and Allen came to pick me up, you quipped perversely.

"Verily, verily I say unto ye . . . I would like to stay at home instead of going to this dinner . . . Now . . . enjoy yourselves, I beseech ye, because I'll be doing the same."

This phrase of yours whirled around my head all night, and I realized, with displeasure, that I was still jealous of you, that I was still tied to you.

I tried to dismiss the thought. I even thought about Sonny Morebugs: what pleasure could there be in letting him screw you?

Often disappointed drunken wives would ring his bell and let themselves be laid in the sauna. Later they would confess to him that they had done it only to revenge themselves on their husbands. "It doesn't matter," Sonny would reply, "if that's the cure you want, it's all right with me too, thanks."

So I, too, thought of him. But your phrase was stronger.

After the movie, when I was again alone in the house, I thought I was going crazy. To be sure, you were with the Ph.D. candidate. What if you were with Rose, instead? No, Rose was still in Florida for the Easter vacation. But Evelyn was in town . . .

Yes, I tormented myself. All this torment because I no longer had any trust. I then remembered a conversation I had in the library with Gee Jay. His affair with Pauline, the wife of that poor wretch, Professor J.J. De Pepperoy, had ruined his marriage with Virginia. And although they still lived together, just as you and I still do, Virginia's problem with Gee had become identical with my problem with you.

"When you love," Gee had said, "you are dealing with one person. When something happens that breaks that oneness you are compelled to deal with two persons."

I cited this utterance of Gee to you and you pronounced it important, indeed "very important," but with the cutting edge of your irony.

You quickly found refuge in the language of ideas which you employ when it suits your convenience as well as for the purpose of better embarrassing your conversational partner, of making him suspicious, of provoking him, and then leaving him in a corner like an old rag.

You spoke with Pythagoras, saying that Gee's wife, poor girl, cannot grasp the concept that oneness is the first numerical entity from which all the other numbers derive, and in which all the opposite properties of numbers, the unequal and the *equal*, are also reunited. You explained that two was the first equal number, whereas three is the first *unequal* number, and as such perfect. (How I hate professors!)

You further explained that the beginning, the middle and the end exist in number three. You spoke of three as if it were God's cipher book! And, instead, all you wanted to say was that Virginia, the betrayed wife, should have accepted Pauline as a necessity, just as I should accept Rose: a middle that continues to tie you to me but which, at the same time, forms an equilateral triangle, or am I mistaken?

Yes: it forms a trestle.

I waited for you in my overcoat with the bottle of Scotch and the cigarettes beside me. I was watching TV, but I saw nothing. I needed its hum in the void, people came and went on the screen, talked, and I felt as if I were wrapped in a blanket. After one o'clock, when the transmissions end (at least on the channels we have), what would I have done still wearing the overcoat? Would I have begun to phone people far away?

Suddenly you came back before one o'clock, thanked up and merry but upon seeing me in the overcoat and looking upset alongside the bottle of scotch and the cigarettes, your facial expression sobered.

"Have you been with Evelyn?"

"No such luck! What's bugging you?"

"I'm going to find myself a lover, do you know that?"

This remark made you explode. You threw your glasses against the TV just as you had done with your typewriter on that other night of crisis (so many crises in only a few days!), wanting to destroy precisely those things that were vital to you, that is your real, true self.

I didn't want this. I tried to stop you, I picked up your glasses, I took you in my arms, but you were stubborn and desired no contacts. You tried to extricate yourself from my grasp and, by so doing, your elbow hit my nose which immediately began to bleed. Then you locked yourself up in the bathroom. When I came into the bathroom to fetch a towel in the mirror I saw a tear-stained, bloody, sad and ugly face, and I saw you, sitting on the toilet seat, looking very distressed, no longer knowing what to do with yourself.

I felt a deep sadness for the two of us. I waited for you. I tried to embrace you in bed. I needed comfort. I needed love. You paid me back in a fogged and vindictive manner. It had been different at other times, it had been natural. But now it struck me as a sadistic act of violence, frigid in the extreme, because you turned me around with a rude impatience so as to sodomize me, and when I rebelled you rejected me with such force that I fell off on the other side of the bed.

Oh, Simon, it's so sad not to love one another anymore.

15

Today is Sunday, and yesterday we spent a pleasant Saturday evening together: you, me, and the Spirit. Did I say pleasing?

No, unusual.

In fact, I no longer know what is normal and what is abnormal. Nor do I care. I'm caught up in the wave, I'm swimming with difficulty, and I'm only trying to keep my head above water. Our quarrels are repeated with an ever greater frequency, and if a day goes by smoothly it seems that I'm almost missing something.

We had quarreled again Friday night because of now uncontrollable jealousy. Finally, in order to get away from me, you said, "I'm going to work at the office."

Perhaps it was true, but to me it sounded like a new excuse to meet Rose.

I replied, "If that's really the case, let's go together, I'll study in the library."

"Are you thinking about Rose?" you replied.

"I don't care about her anymore," I lied. "You could even invite her to the Canaxa. Won't you offer me a drink?"

"Now what are you plotting? Why do you want to invite Rose?"

"I'd like to get to know her better, talk with her . . . "

You shook your head. Then, still mistrustful, you wrote her number on a piece of paper.

"If that's the way it is, call her up yourself, tell her: 'Welcome back, darling, would it displease you to make love with me and my husband, tonight?'"

Impulsively, I slapped your face. I hit you so hard that your glasses fell to the floor, fortunately without breaking. You grabbed me by the wrists, twisting them:

"Have you really gone bunkers?"

"Excuse me."

"O.K. We'll do as you wish. We'll go to the very bottom of the matter."

"What bottom and where?"

"To the bottom of Hell!"

We drove as far as the Ten Thousand Plaza for a hamburger, then he went to his office and I made my way to the library. Students were yawning over their books. The light was clear and artificial, spread enormously as during daytime, but now it had a strange emptiness. It appeared menacing and motionless on the armchairs, on the heads of the students, on the lazy cloud of cigarette smoke, on the walls, on the abstract paintings.

The Art Department painters had neither a name nor a face, nevertheless, they managed to get their paintings hung a little everywhere, in the library, or in the lecture halls.

We had known very many artists but on this campus (at least for me), they all appeared to be apersonal. Of course, it's not true. One tends to belittle when one believes to know better. Or, perhaps, the judgment stems from the fact that we all know each other somewhat — and by hurting, knifing, we think of being friendly sincere, no offense intended.

Simon's glass house was ridiculed, yet admired.

"Are you a kind of Alberti?"

"I'm no architect," he used to answer.

"Are you a kind of Vermeer?"

"I only want to use my hands."

Once I said to him: "This glass house is obscene."

"No," he said. "It's imperfect."

"Obscene!"

He said: "Look, when Mies went to see Philip Johnson's *Glass House* in New Canaan he thought that the workmanship was bad, the design was bad, every thing was bad. Yet I like Philip Johnson's *Glass House* . . . And I like this one too, because it's mine. I made it with my hands. It is not sordid, it does not depend on anybody and, besides, it was built with my money."

If provoked, he can be really obnoxious.

Vanni Webbers, the swaggerer of New York, came to see us one day. He did not act smart about our glass house. He simply repeated what Lloyd Wright said in walking through the front door of Philip Johnson's *Glass House:* "Should I take my hat off or leave it on?"

He took off his trashy trousers. Upon seeing the paintings in the library, he bluntly observed: "They are certified fakes."

This remembrance led me to examine those paintings more attentively, and I was especially struck by one. It depicted a vast blue sky, a variant of shadings of sky. It was so authentic that it looked like an enormous enlargement of a photograph.

A tiny seagull was visible very high in that sky. The sea was not visible but I felt its presence instantly in the invisible depth. I was suddenly assailed by a nostalgic desire to leave, to live for a moment, or forever, far from this library, from this city.

I drew closer to it and read the painter's name: G.O.

So G.O. could actually do something, aside from the cut-off hand, aside from whoremongering, aside from the drugs that he took. Simon had characterized him as a Judas in one of his films. G.O. evinced satisfaction with the characterization since he had no pretensions. He hated polemics and what he yearned for most of all was to get out of the province and to make enough money to retire to his home at Tortola, in the Caribbean. The inspiration of this painting no doubt came from there.

I tried to imagine the island of Tortola, to see myself in G.O.'s house which I would have rented and to re-live the island that I dreamt as a girl when I read that strange book, *The Virgin under the Lion.*

The heroine was a girl of my age, thirteen or fourteen. Walking alone on the deserted beach, she always thought that it would be mysteriously perfect to lose her virginity on that beach.

One day a fisherman emerged from the sea with two enormous shells. The girl thought that if she would stretch herself out on the sand and close her eyes, he would take her with the swiftness and naturalness with which he had taken those shells. The fisherman stopped alongside her. She saw his bare feet and his legs, then she turned around and wrote on the sand: "Knock on my window."

On the next morning, at dawn, the fisherman tossed a pebble against the window of her bungalow. She came out and walked towards the beach. The man followed her. Then she stretched out on the sand, and the man did likewise, at first some distance from her and, after a little while, he moved directly alongside her. They didn't say a word to each other. Finally the man mounted her. He then went away, and she did likewise.

It was only a dream. It was one of those dreams that the girl had never dreamt before. At any rate, she was no longer a virgin, and this was very beautiful.

Every morning the man tossed a pebble against the window of the bungalow. And every morning the girl went down to the beach. She walked and walked, and the fisherman followed her amid the dunes.

When she stretched out on the sand to take the sun, he did likewise. Then he mounted her like the first time because now the morning stroll had become a rite. While the man was on top of her, the girl had a vision of many other girls like herself, whose image reflected on the rocks, as she was being possessed in silence by the lion.

I walked away from the painting vaguely dazed, vaguely in love with myself.

I returned to my seat. My eyes glimpsed the feet and legs of a man, and the man's hand between those legs behind a seat covered with books. I turned my eyes away and saw the girl at a nearby table. She, too, was half hidden behind a pile of books, she looked like Rose. She did not notice the man, and continued her reading.

Rose is a statuesque brunette and her hair, divided into tresses, comes down to her shoulders. I thought that I had been right to accompany Simon. He had come to meet her, and she was waiting for him in the library. It was as simple as that.

She must have felt my eyes on her which were trying to recognize her because she raised her head from the book, looked at me, petrified. And then when she saw the man, she slammed the book shut and ran off among the aisles of bookshelves. She had seen the man who was masturbating while looking fixedly at her. She had also seen me.

I followed Rose, at first at a normal walking pace, but then I too began to run. On the stairs I sighted her red sweater and her black tresses, but then she went through a door which lead to the underground passages. I followed her. She was still running as she entered another door, where I finally lost sight of her, I turned back.

I came to pick you up at the office, and we went back home.

"You know," I said, "there was a man masturbating in the library while he was watching a girl's legs. She was wearing a red sweater and her two black tresses reached down to her shoulders. She looked like Rose."

"Did you talk to her?"

"She noticed me, then the man and now I don't know whether she ran off because of me or the masturbator."

"I've got to phone her," you said, suddenly.

"Why . . . don't you believe me?"

"I'd like to confirm it."

It was, however, already late. We followed the discussions on Watergate on TV. We said nothing about the incident in the library. I went to bed, took a sleeping pill, totally unaware of what you were up to. I saw you only the next morning, Saturday. I was in your arms, we made love, you were inside me with the neatness of a knot, and this was beautiful all over again. My eyes were closed, and I saw myself on the beach of the island with the fisherman mounting me.

16

We had not made love for a few days. My greatest fear was Rose's presence on the campus. Whenever she is around, you put a wall between you and me. But now, miraculously, our bodies were together again as before, as always. I deluded myself. You were still mine; we had the whole weekend during which to enjoy ourselves.

We had dedicated Saturday, Sunday, and Monday to love. I thought of transporting a mattress to the garage so that we could lie there, amid the smell of the gasoline and the spiders.

That was a silly idea. I had no nostalgia for my childhood and adolescence.

Experts would say that we have perfected the art of prolonged coitus, because now you are able to stimulate me to the point where I could achieve long swoonings. The inside of me, which I had always imagined to be reddish-violet in color, made of a soft, gelatinous substance, responded fully to the regular movements of your body. I often felt you soft and silken, delicate to the extreme, like the seagull in G.O's painting. But this time you were very hard, and I recalled the priapism of Vancouver. Only now I laughed. I was happy. For a long time you held the center without oscillating.

We reposed, pleased to know that the day was ours. There would be no visits, no disturbances. The phone was off the hook and the doors were locked. Then you said something that surprised me. "I'd like to make some lasagna today."

You do make them very well, and I do like them very much. You knead and cut the pasta; you prepare the ragu and the ricotta, the eggs and the different cheeses. All the required ingredients were already in the house. But then I thought what if you go out, purchase the goods, sorting them out, opening the door, destroying our intimacy with activity. Moreover, you usually make lasagna when you have guests.

I intuited a plot on your part. Do you see where the loss of trust leads to?

"Did you invite Rose?"

"Rose?"

The description of Rose in the library with the man masturbating as he watched her legs, and I behind her, and you who wanted to phone her for a confirmation of my story, went through your mind and mine, simultaneously, like a lightning flash.

"Weren't you supposed to phone her?" I said. "Invite her, we'll have the lasagna together."

"Are you sure you won't make a scene?"

"Very sure."

After all what unpleasantness could possibly happen? We could spend a tranquil evening as a three some in honor of Pythagoras, and, thank goodness, without outbursts of rage and accusations. And that, I told myself, would have been of great benefit especially to her, Rose, in that she would no longer feel rejected or hated.

But was it really true that I did not reject her, that I did not hate her?

"In that case, you phone her."

"Oh, no, no. You must . . . "

You did phone her. You said that you would pick her up at 3:30 in the afternoon. I objected that it was too early, what would we have done all afternoon and in the evening? Was Rose quick-witted, urbane? I realized that my anxiety was making a comeback. I was silent and, finally, I talked to you about my fears.

"Wasn't that your idea?"

Of course.

Then you said: "What's done cannot be undone. The New System is in progress. According to this new system Teng becomes Deng, and Nanking is Nanjing."

"Would you make love with me and to her at the same time?" I replied, actualizing what you have called the New System.

You laughed, vastly delighted, and asked: "Would you like to make love as a threesome?"

I recalled the time in Judy and Punks' house when Judy and me stretched out on the water bed together with Punks. It was a twosome, initially. Upstairs, you and Judy, were also playing a twosome. Actually there were four of us, it was a foursome. When Judy joined the game and you remained outside, the triad no longer functioned. After Judy's proposal you said, "The fourth player has remained home, sick". And this amazed me. Both you and Punks rejected a foursome. You knew Plato's *Timeo*. Not I, unfortunately. I started reading Jung though without much success.

According to Jung, oneness is simultaneously a triad, and this is linked with femininity. I didn't know its opposite, namely that three, as an unequal number, is masculine. Jung translates the triad directly as maleness. Punks, Judy and me, okay. Judy, me and Simon, okay.

Why Rose?

17

You went out to fetch Rose and came back sooner than I anticipated.

I had expected that you would have lingered in the car to gossip with her, at least for awhile, especially since you had my approval.

Instead, I realized (and this was another surprise) that there was only a relationship of quiet, amicable fusion between the both of you, and that neither of you play games — like mailing recondite allusions or formulating phrases to fit occasions.

Rose struck me as a normal student, deferential but not distant. I must admit, for the first time, that your figure suggested to me the image of the professor in slippers, cordial and relaxed, talkative and spontaneous, one more to make gentle fun of as the archetypical academic rather than one to admire as a male or seducer. You were homespun and alien to arrogant airs, and often amusingly and pleasantly jocose. With just a few touches you had managed to create the right atmosphere, so much so that I no longer felt like a stranger, or defenseless, vis-à-vis Rose.

A strange calm came over me.

We prepared the lasagna together, chattering, laughing, exchanging jokes and quips. We seemed to be old friends, of the kind between whom everything has been already said and every thing has been experienced in common. The kind of friends whom (apart from Punks and Judy) we have never had. I felt like kissing and embracing Rose and, if the moment suggested it, even to disrobe before her, to let her see how I was built, slim and sweet, sister and mother.

Now she had a strange fascination for me. She had undressed and she had laid down with you, and yet it seemed to me that both of you had hardly grazed each other. Her anatomy aroused my curiosity. I observed the curves of her body, the big mouth, the house-wifely arms, and I tried to imagine what her effusions and reactions during the love act would be like. The thought excited me, and from it I distilled a pleasure alternating between languor and aggressiveness.

A forgotten image took shape before me, but it was not distinct or authentic, and that image could have been a configuration of you and me.

Do you remember the trip to the city of San Gimignano, years and years ago, when you were the guest of your publisher in Siena?

A twelfth-century fresco, attributed to Niccolò di Segna, stamped itself on my consciousness. It was a nuptial scene. The bride and groom were seated in a tub of water; her right hand rested on his shoulder, washing it, while he placed his left hand between her legs, washing them. They did not appear to be saying a word to each other. They just looked at each other. On the left side, some distance from them and not looking at them, was their handmaiden, arms outstretched, as if to protect them from strangers.

I had a sudden desire to make love with you in front of Rose (the handmaiden), in a tub even here in the kitchen, savoring the voluptuous smell of the gravy simmering in the pots. Instinctively, I unbuttoned my blouse, my breast emerged in all its whiteness, and I felt I was leaving pink bruises on my neck as I touched it.

Then I said: "Yesterday a girl in the library fled from a man who was masturbating while looking at her." I looked at Rose, our eyes met. "The girl fled along the underground passages and I followed her, I thought I knew her, but she vanished in the tunnels."

"Why did you follow her?" you asked.

"I really don't know."

Then Rose, blushing, said:

"I was the girl."

"That's what I thought," I said.

"I ran as fast and as far as I because a woman was following me. If I had recognized you, I would have stopped, and I would have broken into tears."

"Why would you have broken into tears?"

"I felt a hatred for that man."

I went up to her and embraced her. She was soft, very soft, but tense. "You know, Rose . . . I had planned to hate you. I can't anymore. Do you believe me?"

"It does one good to be forgiven . . . you're a good person."

"No, I'm exclusive. This is my not-so-good side. Instead, it would be necessary to share."

"Share what?" you asked, looking up from the gas-range.

"Love, darling!"

"How about sharing a game of frisbee in the meanwhile?"

"And the lasagna?" Rose added.

"Let's go," and I accompanied her towards the meadow. "We have the whole afternoon and evening before us. I'm really very glad that you came, you know that, I hope?"

"Me, too."

The afternoon slowly evolved into evening. We had played frisbee on the wet grass, joking, laughing, kidding each other. And you were the silliest of all, Simon. Two women were enamored of you, and you tried to make yourself look ridiculous. At a certain point Rose, over-heated, flopped down on the wet grass and said that she had seen the god Pan running through the woods..

"The god who?"

I, too, flopped down on the wet grass and rolled around in it.

"Shall we undress him?" I suggested to Rose.

"Let's!" she agreed.

You had the round dance in mind. Matisse's *Round Dance*, you said. But this required that all three of us be nude. As we were going through the motions of the round dance in the rain we blocked you, tearing off your shirt and your shorts, leaving you naked under the rain, your hands protecting the shadow between your legs. Rose and I went back to the house, padlocking the door, directing obscene gestures your way, and making ugly faces at you from the glass panes. We let you in only when we noticed that you were shivering.

"I'm going to bed," you said. "Is anyone going to follow me?"

Together we followed you to the bathroom, we rubbed you dry very thoroughly. You were laughing, excited.

"What are you two doing to me? What are you looking for?"

We were pretty much wet ourselves by now, but Rose did not want to undress.

"I'm all right, but I'm hungry!" she said.

I went into the bedroom and slipped on my pajamas.

"Rose," I called out.

She came in, helped me arrange my hair, and then I said to her, "Do you know that Simon wants the both of us?"

"No, I don't believe that," she replied.

"You'll see."

The lasagna were delicious despite the can of red peppers that you had added to the gravy, thinking they were peeled tomatoes!

We were seated on the rug around the low glass table, enjoying the food and the wine, the candle light and the music. We had done lots of drinking. A warm feeling of pleasure and satisfaction enveloped us lovingly like a blanket. You had lit the fireplace. The music was night jazz, soft and hyper-scrutable. The rain still beat against the glass panes, but it was cozy inside! Eyes closed, I stretched out on the rug and, once again, I surrendered myself to my dreams.

On the deserted beach in Tortola, in the Caribbean, there was a girl of my age in a bikini.

She said to me: "Uranus has entered the realm of Scorpio. For the next fourteen years we will have an increase in homosexuality."

"No, I'll go under the rainbow," I replied.

"I'll become an hermaphrodite."

"Impossible," she said. "You're too much of a whore. You will never be able to love a woman."

"I'd be able to do anything," I said. "See? I'm water."

"No, you're spring."

"Look," I tried to make her understand, "my personal history is simple. My father is not my father, but a man who my mother married in order to carry out certain roles. My mother conceived me on the high seas with a sailor who later died. She once showed me his photograph, dressed in officer's uniform. At first she said he was her cousin, a distant cousin, and later she told me that he was my father. A strange, distant father. And the one so young! If I looked backward, however, I saw Prick in his sandals, big around the midriff like a pregnant woman, but he was tall and bent, wore glasses and was always looking for a book. I didn't have girl friends when I was growing up. The faces that I knew were those of the Catholic nuns of New Canaan. Often I didn't go to the nursery school, preferring to sit on the station platform, watching the incoming and outgoing trains."

"You already had a body," she said. "Sex is hidden precisely in a train."

"No, no, it sits on the handle bars of bicycles," I said, and I added: "But that wasn't love. My kind of love is something that involves the whole body, not only a precise point of the body on which to draw, into which to enter with the pencil — I also dreamed of the other person (there was another person) who also had a pencil and who began to draw and who then put that pencil in that center which was me."

"Of what love are you talking about? I'm Rose, Rose, do you hear me?"

I took her hand and placed it on my breast. It was as light as a wing, and when it stopped I felt it was like something dead.

"Love is in dreams and sex is in life," I said, resting my hand on her hand that was resting my breast. "In life no sexual act is similar to another sexual act. I'm evolutive, giving, and receptive."

"I'm contemplative," she said. She opened my eyes with two fingers. "Do you see me?"

Her face was directly over mine. We kissed. Then, with a ready laugh, we looked at you next to the fireplace, in your very serious yoga position, watching us as if we were objects in a museum.

"I feel like some ice cream," I said. "Do we have any ice cream?"

"Sorry, no," you answered from your distant corner, shaking your head.

"I'll go get some," Rose volunteered.

Outside it was windy, raining, and cold. It seemed that spring had no intention of arriving that year. But she went out taking the key to our car. Why had I asked for ice cream? Why did I let her go, and not Simon? I wanted to punish her. I didn't want to punish her. On the contrary! Yet I was satisfied by her departure. I was almost patronizing Rose. Perhaps she loved me. I mean to say that, perhaps, she also loved me. And this gave me relief, a sense of belongingness.

From the void came your voice: "You know that this kind of talk is damaging to me. The more you insist on this threesome, the more I dwarf myself. I become the fourth player."

"Weren't you the one who first looked around for a threesome?"

"Number three stands for dissolution, darling. Mine, of course."

"You make me feel guilty," I admitted.

She came back soaked, but visibly pleased to have done something. Perhaps she had felt a real need to estrange herself from herself, to change her body and the thoughts in her brain in the rain, and to think things over, as well. I took her by the arm and accompanied her to the bathroom. I rubbed her down with a towel, dried her, and then left her alone by the mirror where she began to comb her hair.

"Hurry up," I said, "the ice cream is waiting for us."

We ate the ice cream around the fire, and we smoked another cigarette. Billie Holiday was recounting her sad story in a blues number. We were all getting bored. I proposed to re-accompany Rose home. I added, "You can also sleep here . . . in the small glass room area."

I blushed. And I understood that she understood. In fact, she darted a glance beyond the living area where was the site of the small glass room.

"No," she said. "I'm waiting for a phone call from my father."

So I put on my overcoat and we escorted Rose to the dormitory.

"There'll be another night," I thought to myself.

The three of us exchanged kisses in the car as if she were going away forever, as she herself put it.

"It was a beautiful evening, thanks."

That night we slept in the small glass room on the old mattress. It was a dream-filled night for me. One dream seemed to be a continuation of the strange dream on the Tortola beach. Now the girl on the beach was Rose, and I was Bes, her mother. You were also there, Simon, but suddenly your tiny shadow began to move, lengthening itself, and you became the fisherman, tall and proud.

When he mounted her and me, together, he had an amputated hand, and I immediately remembered the stumped hand of the dream in New Canaan, but now the hand caressed my face and a whisper in my ear told me to do the same with the other girl, the girl in the bikini. Only the voice was the voice of the bear — yours.

Apart from this, what is strange is that while you were mounting us, you didn't call her intimate recess a cave, but a *temple*.

I wonder why.

18

We had Rose over for supper last night too. It was a last meeting before her return to Utica. I phoned her. She was undecided.

"I've got to tell you about a dream I had. You were in it."

"Me? Why me?"

"So you're coming?"

"Okay."

In the last few days I had been almost totally obsessed by the idea of a *ménage à trois*. I felt a rancor towards myself and towards Simon. I felt him obstinately distant, uncommitted, still vaguely diffident and fearful of my unforeseeable reactions. And, above all, I felt that he no longer trusted me. He was afraid that I might lock him definitely in a situation which he would bitterly regret later. He thought that I was blackmailing him, and it was true. I was blackmailing. For my part, I was staking everything.

I was nervous Monday, Tuesday, and all of yesterday.

Yesterday, after accompanying you to Senator Key's house for a consultation on college matters, I found myself again alone at nine in the morning with no desire whatsoever to work on my thesis. I decided to clean the house again, figuring that some physical work would distract me, by tiring me. It's curious, but in this last crisis-ridden month I've cleaned the house so many times that sometimes I think I've become a slipshod housekeeper.

I had stopped at the Ten Thousand Plaza, at the drug store, to get a supply of cigarettes. As I often do when I've got time to kill, I stopped to browse at the paperback bookshelf. It's incredible how much stuff is being put out by the publishing industry, especially in the matter of books dealing with sex.

At last I found the book I was looking for. It was an anthology of letters written to a well-known magazine, *Sex Forum*. Frank and confessional, the letters covered a great variety of erotic experiences, from lesbianism to sperm-swallowing. It had an index, so I immediately looked up the term *ménage à trois*. It was there, but it explained nothing. It suggested another text as reference. Disappointed, I was about to return the book in its place when my attention was drawn to the word *troilism* which I did not know but which described exactly that type of threesome experience which had been in our consciousness since last Saturday night.

There were letters *pro* and *con* troilism. I thus discovered that my reactions, during Saturday night, were neither unique nor abnormal. The *voyeur* element is shared by all those who enjoyed this type of encounter. It is sexually and mentally exciting, especially for that mind in search of a renewal of routine living.

According to the doctor who edited the collection, there exists in us the unconscious satisfaction of watching other persons make love. It is a satisfaction that derives, so asserted the doctor, from the repressed desire, that has never surfaced before, to spy on our parents in their performance of the sexual act. Often the participants themselves become even more sexually excited when they know that a stranger is present, spying on them. The mirror in a room or on a bed often assumes the personality of a "third" term. Indeed, to see one's own acts in the mirror corresponds to one of the properties of the *voyeur*.

I did not realize up to then that our glass house can be thought of being our ever present "third eye"!

I bought the book and went back home. I was so excited by that reading that I wanted to make love instantly, in front of our rolling and wooded landscape, never used before for this purpose. You were far away, discussing who knows what with the state legislators. I thought of the man in the library, and I thought of Rose.

I impulsively phoned Rose, and I invited her. Then I set to work with a brush and a pail of soapy water, listening to pop music.

You were supposed to phone me around ten o'clock, but the hour passed and there was no ring on the phone. I told myself that the work you were doing had required more time than foreseen and I tried to forget you.

I continued with the house cleaning operations, cherishing the moment when I would stretch myself out in the bathtub. Eventually two o'clock rolled around, and then two-thirty, and the usual fears re-surfaced. I myself had accompanied you to the place of your appointment, but then was it really true that you went there and not elsewhere? And what if you were with Rose? Certainly you were with her when I phoned, and perhaps you had both made fun of me, of this fidgety and police-like wife.

I was seized by a sudden rage, I beat my fists against the floor. Then, suddenly, you called at three and asked me to come pick you up. I got a glimpse of you from the car. You looked sodden and exhausted in the wind that was beginning to blow harder. In fact, you yawned during the ride home.

"This has been one of those days that I call lost forever," you said with a tired smile. "All I want to do is sleep."

"I invited the Spirit to dinner."

"You did?" You made a sudden movement. A new life flowed through your quickened body. You no longer yawned. Then, almost abruptly, you sat back again and in a lamenting tone you said, "But why, why Lisa?"

"I thought it would please you."

"No, I'm fed up . . . I'm fed up with dragging myself in shit, in troubles, in body games. I'm fed up with eating, drinking, fucking morning noon and night, rancid lectures, mean-spirited colleagues, passive students, cold hearts . . . "

"The meeting with Senator Key must have really depressed you."

"It sure did. There was a lady who looked like an owl, in an empty and dusty room with old registers and piles of papers. When I was seated with the others, she stood up behind me, observing my neck. She was so fat and worn-out that I felt my own flesh falling apart. I thought of my eyes. I thought of cigarettes producing cancer. I thought I had syphilis. I thought of a little room in a hospital and of my son Sandro, in Italy, whom I would have urgently sent for, whom I would have begged to bring me a pistol. A pistol for his father, a coward in the face of illness."

"Would you use it?"

"Maybe . . . "

"Who was that woman?"

"Everybody called her Ms. Immortality. She built, after raising money here and there and everywhere, the Public Library of Anabasis, and she has also placed my books on its shelves. She has been the favorite guest of governors and senators. She was also an old flame of H.H., and an adviser to Cardinal Spexs . . . She's a three-time divorcee, and two of her husbands committed suicide following the divorce. As she was observing my neck, I wondered just where the magic might reside in Ms. Immortality's grotesque body."

At home I made him a strong gin-tonic, which he promptly gulped down. After which he had another, took a shower, and changed his clothes.

Then the book caught his eye.

"What's this?"

"It's a gift for you. In it there's a word, *troilism,* that made me buy it."

You leafed through it lazily, then you threw it into a corner. I realized that you had already read it.

"At what time is Rose coming?"

"You have to go pick her up."

"Now?"

"In a little while, yes."

You went out, unwillingly. I, instead, began to amuse myself. I prepared the chicken, I drank another gin-tonic, and when you both came into the kitchen I said, and with an exuberance that surprised me, "How punctual you both are!"

I embraced both of you, kissing her first, on the mouth, and then you.

You said: "Look at that! If I had kissed her you would have accused me of performing an illegal act!"

"Why didn't you then?"

You first kissed me, then her.

Rose, shrugging her shoulders, said, "I've read that polygamy is legal, at least in some areas of Idaho."

"But not sodomy" I said. "That is prohibited all over America."

I realized that, trying to be witty, I had made a stupid and senseless remark but one that, at the same time, established the limits of *our* polygamy. Your face darkened. Making some excuse, you went into the bedroom area, adding that we should call you when dinner was ready.

Or did you simply want to leave her alone with me?

We sat down at the kitchen table, drinking gin-tonics. Rose was wearing a dowdy dress, a bit babyish, which was very fashionable among students. Nevertheless she was very well-built, athletic without being hard. An ideal stewardess type!

I asked her about her interview with TWA.

She replied, "Depressing."

I asked her about her family, about her father and mother, and about the boy she had planned to marry. She had even bought a trousseau. But then the marriage never took place.

Why?

"Because of my virginity," Rose said. "I was afraid."

"Me, too, but of my mother."

"I was afraid of my father." This was followed by a reflective pause, then Rose added: "No, it's not that exactly. I wasn't afraid of him, but of his trust. He always had such great trust in me, in that matter. Every time I came back from somewhere his eyes x-rayed me. He spoke very little. What did you do with Sinbad? Did you enjoy yourself? And I knew the answer that he wanted."

"Do you love your father very much?"

"He's super."

"More than your mother?"

"I also love her, but he's super." I didn't understand. Then she added, "When we were little, my sister and I, she always attacked him. But my father always was silent, patient . . . "

I studied her. How different Rose would be today if she had followed her impulse. If she had given herself to Sinbad instead of respecting the paternal law! She would have never entered my life. She would be a mother and wife now. Instead, she had reduced herself to the experience of the mature man, stealing.

Hadn't I also done the same?

I had decided to lose my virginity with Simon, knowing very well that he was married with two children. Then I dragged him along with me. I still insist with myself that I did not steal Simon from Sibyl. He loved me. He had wanted it. Or do I imagine all these things in self-justification?

I don't know. I know only that I would not have him taken away from me by Rose, because I would have left him first. Perhaps this is why I wanted the three-some relationship, so that I could build an alibi for myself. And in this way nobody would have robbed from anybody. Hell, of course, would welcome us with joy, but together.

Then, without looking at me, she said: "I'm worry over what happened between me and your husband."

"Do you love him?"

"I don't know . . . and you?"

"I don't know, either. The difference between you and me is that I'm his wife, and this makes it more a matter of pride than of love. But I believe I still love him . . . "

"I'm sorry. You are a good person."

"No, not at all. At first I felt offended. Now I'm no longer offended. On the contrary, look, I'm glad that we've talked about it."

"And the dream?"

"Ah, the dream." And I blushed. "Okay, I'll tell it to you. I was on a beach with you and him, and he made love with you and then with me. Isn't that horrible?"

"No," she said, and smiled. She reached out a hand and took mine. "You know," she said, "one time I also had a dream. I was with him and he was with another woman. I don't remember her face, but certainly it was you. And I was happy, I swear, and in harmony with the whole world."

I got up. The chicken was ready to serve now. All that remained to be done was to kindle a log in the fireplace, and wake up the *pascià*. I said, "You go call him."

She laughed.

"If I go alone, he'll grab me. If we go together he'll grab us together . . . "

"You know him so well."

"No, I don't. But I do know one thing. When he wants something, there's no stopping him . . . "

We entered the bedroom area on tip-toe. You were sleeping like Duke Alexander de' Medici in Guicciardini's description.

"Lord, are you sleeping?"

Uttering these words, I stabbed him with a dagger (a long-stemmed carnation which I had taken from the looking-glass), and passing it from side to the other of his body.

The duke, after receiving so grievous a wound, rolled backwards on the bed and, thus rolling, he slipped down from the rear of the bed and attempted to escape, shielding himself with the book on troilism which he had taken with him. Rose dealt a knife-thrust to his face (it was the broken stem of another carnation), and slashing one of his temples she cut a great part of his left cheek.

Meanwhile, Lisa, who had pushed him back on the bed held him there on his stomach. She pressed herself down on him with all her might, while keeping a hand over his mouth to prevent him from shouting. The duke, helping himself as much as he could, bit her so hard and angrily on her forefinger that Lisa, who by now had saddled herself on him completely, could not strike him with the flower-dagger. She called out to Rose for help.

Rose ran here and there about the room, and being unable to wound Simon without wounding Lisa first, or at the same time. At best she could pierce only the straw mattress. But finally she took recourse of a knife which she happened to have on her person (it was a hairpin) and, grazed the duke's throat. She jabbed at it again and again until it was properly cut.

After he was dead, she inflicted still another wound on him as a result of which he shed so much blood that it flooded almost the whole glass house.

What was noteworthy in all this was that for the whole time that Lisa held him firmly underneath her, and for the hole time that he saw Rose run from the front to the rear of the bed, and vice versa, exploring ways to kill him, he never complained or made an attempt to shake her off his back; nor did he make any effort to release the finger that he had lovingly seized between his teeth.

Finally, exhausted after that unexpected struggle, I said: "Lord, are you dead?" And I ran to the brick cylinder to wash up.

19

We sat down on the rug to dine.

As a scientist, Simon, you tend to perceive reality in symbolic terms, attaching great importance to details. You know very well the difference that exists between the formal atmosphere created by sitting around a glass table and the informality resulting from sitting cross-leg on the rug near the fire, as was your express wish.

The food was tasty. Roast chicken in a stew of peeled tomatoes, garlic and parsley, and *risotto alla Milanese*, suffused with saffron. We ate slowly, enjoying everything, talking of usual and casual things. Rose asked you why you were so interested in watching TV without sound.

I replied: "According to him, a comic film assumes form on the screen . . . and we ourselves can provide the missing dialogue."

"Curious, I must say," she commented.

After the meal was over, I quickly cleaned up, piling the plates in the washing machine. Usually I washed them right away, but now I wanted to stay with you and Rose, without leaving you alone for a minute. When I returned I found you both stretched out on the Peruvian stole, sipping wine, silent, gazing at the fire. You had put Coltrane on the record player, but very low, absorbitive. The sensual flows of the other Saturday were not yet present, despite the kisses on open mouths that had ushered in the evening, and despite the battle on the bed that had taken place a short time earlier which you had defined as an attempted homicide on the part of both of us — your women.

Now I was looking for a triggering cause, and finally I said:

"I bought a new dress, do you want to see it?"

You jumped up, surprised.

"A new dress? When did you buy it?"

"When I went shopping with Kate, do you remember that day she came to your office and when she commented that she very much liked my choice?"

You didn't remember. Yet Kate had made a terrible gaffe because the choice of the dress was a secret. I wanted to prepare you before telling you about it, waiting for the right moment. And you, distractedly, replied: "Yes, the jacket is really beautiful."

You were referring to an ensemble that I had bought two weeks before. Kate understood and, together, we laughed about the risks of life when secrets of no real importance can cause apprehension and misunderstandings. You, on the other hand, had initiated a new economic plan for the house hold budget, and I was afraid of an angry outburst.

I said to Rose: "It's a white jersey, very sexy. You'll like it too."

"Can it be seen?" she asked, and, together we stared at you.

"Oh, let's all take a look at the very sexy jersey."

"Shall I bring it out here and try it on?"

"Put it on."

Happy, I went to change. I removed my shirt and pants. I undressed completely, keeping on me only my panties, soft and thin, a strip of silk at best. You yourself had advised me to buy them. Even though at first I had felt insulted by your suggestion, figuring that you wanted to dress (and undress me) as you had probably done with other women, I was now satisfied with bikinis.

A woman, I told myself, must always try to appear sexually fresh to her man, if she wants to keep him in bed over the years. It was now thirteen years that we had been sharing a bed together. I also removed my bra in order to slip on the new dress. It was truly stupendous, very daring, chic and designed deliberately to set a woman's body in bold relief. Made of a close-fitting texture, the dress wrapped itself around the body, emphasizing the curves. The most notable detail was the open-neck, so low it was useless to wear the bra. I did not see myself as a Scarlett O'Hara, but that dress did so much for me that I could have competed with any other girl, including Rose.

When I came into the living area barefoot, aware of being sexually desirable, I saw you both on your knees in front of the fire, you with your arms on her shoulders and she with hers on yours.

"Here I am for you . . . Am I disturbing?"

I felt the scratch of jealousy return.

"It's really cute," Rose said. "It looks very well on you."

You got up and lit a cigarette. Finally, with a worried expression on your face, you said, "So this is the dress?"

"Don't you like it?"

"No, that's not it."

"It's one of the few occasions when having tiny tits is an advantage."

"I can see that very well. But with that kind of an outfit, you're looking for a lover. You didn't buy it to keep a husband."

Rose and I protested.

"You don't like it."

You laughed: "I'm wondering why you said that it looked good only on tiny-titted women. Wouldn't it look good on Rose?"

Such a remark would have irritated me on any other occasion. Rose herself interjected: "Are you crazy? There's nothing more personal than a dress."

"Okay. Didn't we agree that, at least tonight, each one of us was entitled to do what he or she pleased? If you don't want to try it on, Rose, that's entirely up to you."

Rose looked at me questioningly.

"He's right," I said. "Let's put on a fashion show for him."

I had another sexy outfit which I had bought last year for the trip to Italy and which you, Simon, considered so provocative that could lead to a street riot. I proposed that I wear that one, and Rose the other. Rose agreed and this gladdened me; the evening was unfolding in the desired direction. We went into the bedroom area carefully rolling the moving canvas behind us, at this point such a precaution was rather silly.

I took off my dress, shamelessly displaying my body, totally naked except for the bikini. I observed her to see if she was observing me while she slowly undressed. I was also curious to see the body of the girl with whom you had made love.

Her legs were robust and nervous, like those of a ballerina. Rose did take dance lessons. Her body was very beautiful, shapely, full and hard, whereas I was fragile, bony and slim, almost diaphanous. The only way I could show off an attractive body was to preserve its slenderness to excess, while Rose, with the years, would have to face the perils of pregnancy which leaves certain zones of the body flabby, while puffing up others.

I put on the dress that you had considered too far out for Italy. The gown was long and pleated, made of printed silk. Its novelty consisted in the top piece, a small pea-colored jersey held together by two laces, one around the neck, the other around the waist. Inside it I appeared nude. Rose put on the new dress I had bought. It looked good on her. The whiteness of the material contrasted violently with her dark, almost swarthy complexion.

We came into the living area on tip-toe, as if flying on a gangway, offering ourselves to your eyes and your judgment, summarized in your comment: "I was right, it goes well only with tiny tits."

Rose protested: "But I'm not big-titted!"

You drew closer to us to kiss Rose's breasts, and then mine.

"See, Simon," I said, "You're confused, you don't know what you want."

"It's true. Abundance blinds me, like food, so I end up eating nothing at all."

We returned to the bedroom, again carefully rolling the moving canvas behind us. Rose got back into her own clothes so quickly that I barely noticed her putting on her bra and her panties which were long, white and girlish — looking like laced-edged shorts. They masked the whole lines of her body. I, instead, dressed myself slowly, perhaps in order to be better observed by Rose, or maybe because I sensed that you would be coming soon.

I was lounging between the chest of glass drawers and the bed, when you came in. I saw you through the glass walls. I noticed that when Rose was about to put on her dress you tore it out of her hands.

"It's not here," you said. "Why don't you stay as you are? We can relax next to the fire, and even imagine we're on a beach."

Rose surprised me by instantly consenting to the proposal without uttering a word. She returned to the living area in her over-sized panties, and I did the same in my bikini. We stretched out on the Peruvian stole with you, fully dressed, in the middle, scrupulously avoiding to touch us. Then, suddenly, pulling on the elastic band around Rose's panties, you said:

"Why don't you take them all off? Let's imagine we're on a nudist beach. I was on one in Senegal. Nudity quenches desire."

"No, no" she protested. "The panties are a must to me if I want to survive this night."

I laughed, because it was true: pure like a virgin on her nuptial night!

"I'm going to take my shirt off at least. Do either of you mind?"

"You can take everything off, if you like," I said, and closed my eyes.

You were next to me and Rose, in shorts yourself now. I had one hand on her, the other on me. Then you pulled my hand towards the center of your body. You also drew her hand to the same spot, and her hand grazed my hand. But she withdrew hers instantly, as if scorched.

"You really don't want to take everything off?"

"I'm fine the way I am, thank you," she replied in an irritated tone. Then she turned around and lay down on her stomach, hiding her head between her arms.

I've read that polygamy is legal, at least in some areas of Idaho.

But not sodomy. That's prohibited all over America.

"You two do whatever you please, I'm going to sleep," she said.

You stared at me.

"Do you want to?"

"Yes."

My body, my mind, and my nerves were excited to a fever pitch. I was conscious of the fact that something very strange was taking possession of me. I wanted you to make love with me, but at the same time I wanted you to start off with her. In fact, you turned towards her, laying a hand under her belly, trying once more to pull off the elastic band around her panties. But she stirred, visibly annoyed, pressing her body even harder against the Peruvian stole and her hands even more closely against her head. Then, discouraged, you again stretched yourself out between the two of us, and said:

"The same rite has been repeated after so many years. I was ten years old when, for the first time, I perceived that a girl was made for love. This girl used to sleep beside me in the hay-loft in Selimo during the trashing time in our countryside. Worn out, the men and the women slept and snored in the darkness of the hay-loft, but she and I held our breaths. When I whispered to her to take off her tiny underpants, she said, 'Pull the lace.' Despite the darkness, I found it immediately. It was a chance. I mounted her, but remained absolutely still, I didn't have a hard-on. I had nothing. It was as if I were on a bridge, and she was the water. Then I realized that I was afraid. What if those around us should wake up? They could have killed me with their pitchforks. I dismounted her and fell asleep. On the next day, in the sunlight, I avoided her eyes and she mine, but we flirted with each other by playing hide and seek behind the trees. We had tried to do something so much bigger than ourselves that in the light of day we were ashamed of ourselves, though knowing that henceforth we were bound to each other by a secret."

Then you got up, slipped off your shorts, and threw them into the fire. I glimpsed at your nakedness, and I saw the flame. You were wholly bent over the flame, as if you wanted to immolate yourself. I shouted, "Come back here between us, have you gone crazy?"

Rose also turned around and saw you nude.

"What are you doing?"

"Get up," I told her, "give me this."

I gathered up the stole and threw it over you, pulling you away from the fire.

"I'm going to bed," you said, and disappeared in the bedroom area.

Rose and I remained alongside the fire. I took her hand and pressed it. We remained thus alongside the fire, silent, until very late, until the coal in the fireplace turned to ashes. I began to feel cold. It was a feeling of fatigue. I said to Rose:

"Let's go see the scoundrel."

We went into the darkened room and slipped under the bed sheets, she on one side of you, I on the other.

Your body gave off a smell of burning.

Later that night, with the moon shining, you went out on the wet meadow and started digging a grave.

20

The pep-pills are finished.

I stop reading and put the radio on. An anxious and distant voice, that of a commercial, shouts: " Mrs. Jones, oh Mrs. Jones. Next time use Mop and Glo . . . "

No, no more Mop and Glo, Mrs. Jones. This house is up for sale.

Now it's late, it's late. The last bus from New York will arrive at one in the morning. Maybe she'll be on it. She'll take a taxi, or maybe she'll call and ask me to pick her up.

It has been a torrid day, and I need the rain, instead, to be in the woods like that time, years ago, up on Caribou Creek, under hemlocks, or Kildare Harbour, Kitimat, Kemano Harbour, Klewnuggit Inlet, Mitchell Cove, Upper Kitlope River, Shinnish Creek, Oyama when I signed up one summer with the Forest Service in B.C., Canada, to do some research with the woodsmen along with my assistant Pier. The rain was a fine mist falling from very high clouds, almost blue in the nights, falling on the surface of the inlet with singing sound like the muffled chirping of millions of crickets, and Lisa was only a mute call in my mind.

She chose to take a summer off and travel across Europe with her mother. I went up north to see the bears, to be killed for sure. I missed her and wanted her, but all I received was rain and cold.

I can no longer remember how I felt at Hope. I was out for two weeks with Pier, in the rainy weather, wet in my sleeping bag.

Nights of agony, days of a gray, zombie-like trance, lost in a sort of gray fog, loss of time, the rain was even passing through me, through my mind, with Lisa in my mind, the waterfalls — God's grandeur — in my ears, while the rivers — with their strong currents, back-eddies, log-jams, protruding snags, junctions of streams with their sudden changes of current and water level — most murderous, under my boots.

Yet I loved waterfalls and rivers. Even I loved the snow, wet, cold, and deathly. At times, sitting within a cloud under a piece of canvas, twelve feet by twelve feet, with no sides, stretched between three trees and a log, I felt strangely calm and comfortable. But the nights were never entirely quiet around there. There was always the sound of water coming off the rocks. Black flies, often harmless, fly around my face like a series of permanent spots in front of my eyes. But they never bit me.

Now I can't even remember the kind of despair I felt for not being able to write in the insistent rain, for not being able to love. I searched for branches, roots, leaves, blades of grass and then clung onto the log trying to pull myself out the insane Kitlope River. The current was washing me under the log, my hands and head on the upper side. The river did not feel cold, was almost warm, embracing. "Let yourself go." Yes. "Allow yourself to be carried away by the soft water." Yes.

Now it rains again, the rain is falling harder, its sound on the water is a low whistle.

"This is a different rain," said Pier. "The coastal rain is very much different from that of the interior."

Yes, I know.

There, in the interior, thunder storms are terrifying, the rain falls hard for awhile, then stops. Here, there are no storms, the rain rarely falls hard, and it never stops. It is like a glue which joins the gray sky and the gray sea. Soon it will be difficult to tell one apart from the other, from where the rain will come, which way the rain will fall.

One night in Kitimat it was extremely hot and humid. The deck was covered by a warm dew. The night air was heavy. I thought of Vera Cruz and the Caribbean Coast of Mexico. As we crossed jungle rivers, the air seemed to hang over us like a wet towel. I remember a sunrise on the Coast of Campeche — an orange fireball rising suddenly out of the sea, then climbing over the tops of coconut trees. An orange fireball with no rays no clouds to reflect it, just hanging without support, and slowly rising.

Here's the problem: the sun always reminds me of the cold and how many times I used to get drunk. Lisa was not at home. I would walk home drunk, walking in a gray world, a low gray cloud pressing down against the back of my head. I would think that the world had been telescoped into a gray sidewalk which stretched in front of my feet: an empty gray road on one side, a row of empty mist-shrouded houses on the other side. In my mind a gray cold, a gray fog, a gray Lisa, and in bed, at home, a cold bed.

I remember that sometimes, in my sleeping bag, it would be morning before the cold would finally leave me. The cold was like a disease gripping my legs, my back, my ass, my elbows, but mainly my legs, lingering, keeping the feet for last. It clung tenaciously to me, like a dull ache, like a glacier.

How would you like to freeze to death?

It is a dull, aching feeling, which crawls slowly through the body, until finally it engulfs Lisa, my brain.

The fog lies on the water, along the shoreline, in a strangely flat manner. It pokes delicate tendrils into the valleys, little wisps hang still in the air. They do not seem to move. I look away for awhile, then back: the tendrils have shifted their positions.

To be very tired is to have a dull ache throughout the body, particularly in the arms. To feel as though a brake had been applied to the brain, or that sand has been rubbed into one's eyes.

I remember my first visit to Spokane with Pier. Lisa was still in Europe reading Henry Miller. I was reading Kerouac, writing in my notebook, actually Pier's notebook. I would dictate to him, just as Marco Polo dictated to Rustichello da Pisa his *Milione,* for he was too tired to write, too blind to see. I would stare across the lake, and wonder just what it is that makes this one country and that one another. I would try to see a line on the mountains, some difference between the two, Canada over here, U.S.A. over there.

No difference. Not even in language. The hills of yellow grass and sagebrush stretch their muscles all around the lake. The forest-covered mountains in the far south look the same as those to the far north. Here and there, yellow pine and douglas fir gently roll on hilltops, and further down twist through the crevices between boulder faces. Still lower, the rounded sandy knolls are guarded by a thin line of yellow pine sentries.

Now one hundred miles to Spokane, rolling plains as far as the eye can see, furrowed fields with boulders. Low blue hills suddenly appear in the haze to the north; southward, a regular prairie, a road slicing through the rocks; Grand Coulée dam is down below, enormous, passing weird pockmarked cliffs with light green fluorescent-looking stain; some cliffs are red, maybe lichen, or else weathered metallic ore; a black scar of a burnt-out field; the bus is working hard to climb the rich dark-brown unplanted soil, falling away below us in checkered panorama; rounded furrows along rolling contours; we pass by a terrifyingly high railway bridge; a gas station with large rocks stuccoes on the roof. Astro Tavern. Welcome to Spokane!

Planes are too loud here. Sometimes the ground shakes. I swim though the shallow rapids of Spokane River, diving from a flat rock in midstream over some rocks and into the white water which became a series of waves. I frog-paddle into shore and wade back out to rock again. People are on the beach formed by junction of creek with river. Most are naked, one beautiful girl lies on her back, causing memories of Lisa, who got me lost in the woods, saying, laughing, "Yes, Doc, my Doc, I can still move my tail for you."

In the Wild West Café full of girls I feel somehow empty and jibe. Just had a couple of beers and a small shot of apple wine with a drunk Indian who asked Pier, "Are you an Indian or a China man?" I meet a Meti-German from Alberta who says his Meti father enlisted him in the army when he was eighteen, so he wouldn't have to feed him. He says, "I'd kill you just like that." Then he invites us to go for a ride on his Harley. Pier declines, noticing his legs are no good. He meets a beautiful woman, white hair, past twenty-five, a most unbelievable voice, slightly harsh, country and western, and all of a sudden I feel I'm in no hurry to go anywhere, could stay here forever.

Here there are people from everywhere.

"Glad to help a fellow Texan."

"You can trust him, he's from Alabama."

"South west, man, great place to be from."

"I keep meeting all these California people." A cowboy wino from Calgary gets blotto. An Indian from Cranbrook talks quietly about his jail experiences, Pier stands up twice by women, walks away, and later there is a weird man short hair and two German shepherds, standing around the campfire holding a sleeping bag, while his two beasts sniff in everybody's tent.

"I caught this dude in my sleeping bag, so I kicked him in the head. Went to get my knife so I could stab him, but he'd fucked off. Me and my partner went after him, but we couldn't catch him. Have you ever seen such a nice pair of dogs?"

Pier, later: "One of my favorite hobbies used to be throwing rocks at guard dogs through a fence. I once got attacked by a big white samoyed, right on a city street. It jumped at my throat, but I put up my arm and caught it across the jaw. I gave it a boot."

Later, someone comes to the campfire, where we are drinking beer, and asks if we've seen the guy with the two German shepherds, because he's ripped off his sleeping bag.

"Oh, here's the man with the gallon jug of wine," says a round-faced dark-haired girl. "Did you know that the friends you brought around last night, with all those bottles of booze, busted a couple of friends of mine?"

A man sitting on a stool says, "They told me they were truck drivers when they picked me up on the way to camp, so I offered them a couple of beer. They asked me if there was a party going on at the camp and I said most likely, so they offered to get some more booze. First we cruised past the house of a friend of theirs who was supposed to have some overproof, but he wasn't in. They didn't care for my suggestion that they try an open window. So next we went to Clyde's home. He's the oldest one. We parked in front until he came out with eight half-filled bottles of booze — rum, wine, and liqueurs. I remember mixing them all together in a big coffee liqueur bottle, a couple of times, and passing it around the campfire, then later waking up in my sack. I don't remember anybody being busted."

"Well, they grabbed them just after most people had crashed out."

"What were they busted for?"

"Dealing speed."

"Are they still in jail?"

"Yeah."

As the man on the stool is telling this, there is another man with blond hair and a frizzy beard watching Pier very closely. He calls himself Louisiana, and talks about breaking out of a southern jail.

"A couple of people got hurt, but I wasn't going to spend the rest of my life there. If they ever come looking for me, the trial takes place right here, and there's the river. I ain't going back into no courtroom, and that's for sure."

Louisiana turns to face the round-faced dark haired girl:

"Where are you from?"

"Portland."

We spend a lot of time just sitting around, each of us staring into the fire. Once in a while we sneak a glance at one another.

Pier and I try to make small talk with the girl, but she is not friendly. So we leave and go back to our own camp.

Louisiana shows up later on and informs us that he is convinced the round faced girl is a cop, and so is another guy we turned up with earlier.

"Can I bum a couple of joints off you?" he asks Pier. He gladly give them to him. We do the triple handshake and, before evening has finished arriving, he is gone. "They just don't understand us road people."

Yes, I tell myself now, it has been a torrid day.

Tomorrow night I'll be having a dinner at Norina and Franz's home, the young French professors from California. They are going to stay. She's a lesbian; he's a gay. They will be getting married in September.

The 23rd and the 24th will be registration days in the Gym, students coming and going, professors coming and going, chaos, gossiping, new books, old colleagues, new colleagues, routine, boredom. Lectures will begin on Monday, August the 26, Academic Year of 19 . . . Every thing comes to an end and everything starts all over again.

I love the rain.

Appendix

About Accademia

Man's life as commentary to abstruse,
Unfinished poem. Note for future use.

Nabokov,
Pale Fire

1. Two Old Friends

I wrote this book, *Accademia*, about twenty years ago, perhaps more, when death had positioned itself around my heart, when I became partly, as Petrarch put it, "a man other than what I am."

I went to see an old friend of mine in New York, Dr. Ralph Pépin, a Canadian-born psychoanalyst, with whom I had made a mad journey to the Arctic in 1952, in search of uranium.

We had rented a tin plate plane, tiny and fragile, in Churchill Bay from Moravian missionaries. All we had was a compass in order to take our bearings during the heavy storms, but it was worthless.

They found us after a week, half frozen, amidst mink and muskrat traps.

It was a time when I was trying to decide between going into geology and anthropology as a life-time profession, even though I had already written literary essays and a few novels. Ralph was toying between medicine and law, that is between politics and money.

Ralph Pépin was ruddy, lean, and irascible. But he could remain motionless for hours, like a tree in a public park. And he was heartless.

"I lost my heart somewhere," he told me. "In an old closet. I'll find it again when I'll be needing it."

2. The Number Three

Now I knew that Pépin was in New York. I had found this only after reading an article of his in English, in which he furnished his name and address. Usually he wrote in French. I didn't phone him, though. His brittleness, as I remembered it, awed me.

He hated Freud, lunatically. And he acquired a reputation and lots of merits in Paris, working in Vincennes with Jacques Lacan.

He did not believe in psychoanalysis, and became a psychoanalyst. He espoused Lacan's *École Freudienne* in order to later divorce himself from it and set himself up in New York on Madison Avenue. He related all this in one of his books that I read in French, titled *Non est nom*. Later I read it in English, translated under the title *The Loss of Spontaneity*.

Subsequently, I perceived that Pépin had preserved two characteristics of his teacher Lacan:

a) very brief sessions with the patient;

b) the patient is a somnambulist.

He was sporting a beard now. A red beard speckled with very dirty gray spots that sunk deep into his skin, as found on a leper or a victim of AIDS.

He welcomed me with the gentle opening of Brahms' *Fourth Symphony*. And, following the ceremonious preambles, fixing his topaz-colored eyes on me, he asked me point-blank: "What's the matter with you?"

"I'm obsessed by number three. And I believe that my illness has three names."

"Which?"

"Phallus, castration, desire."

"You have forgotten *jouissance*."

"Precisely. Pleasure or ecstasy would be number four. The fourth element must have remained in bed, sick, together with my genetic identity."

Ralph Pépin laughed. "You talk like Jung," he said.

"This is Plato's *Timeo*," I said.

He turned his red, nay yellow, beard toward the stereo and changed Brahms for the introduction to Mozart's *Eine Kleine Nachmusik*.

"Do you remember that at one time you spoke to me about your heart, that you had lost it somewhere, in an old closet? I would like for you to find it again, because I'm really sick," I said.

"Please, tell me everything."

And I told him everything. In fact, I even cut my recital short after noticing that he was insistently eyeing his wrist watch.

Then he said:

"There's nothing wrong with you."

"What if I kill myself?"

"You've already done so," he said. "That's why there's nothing wrong with you. There's nothing *more* wrong with you."

He accompanied me to the door. Shaking my hand, he said: "You're a writer, uh?"

"I was."

"Do as Svevo did. Write a book on it. Then bring it to me. I'm a collector of manuscripts."

I was furious, but I wrote the book in a few weeks. I signed it using "Anonimo Selimano" as a name.

That was its title and its author: the confession, my confession, was absent from the title as well as the author. I realized this immediately. I had written something that was not "true," not "sincere": culture imposed on nature, identities in fragments, subversion of perception and intent to obscure objectivity, mental and linguistic representation, non ethical, imaginary and not real.

I was ashamed of it, as of a sin.

Another mistake.

3. Nabokov County

Nevertheless I went to see him.

He almost hit me.

"Is that the way you write books? In two days?"

"I know. This book is an imperfect substitution," I replied. "But my anguish is real."

Ralph Pépin snatched the manuscript out of my hands, went behind his desk, and began to leaf through the pages furiously, upsetting them, folding, crossing, and recomposing them. Suddenly, as I observed him from my chair, I saw that he was mixing them with a sliver of his bile.

"Yes: my anguish is real," he said to himself, mockingly. "So Nabokov County is real, uh?"

"Do you remember Yoknapatawpha Country?"

"Vaguely."

"Do you remember *The Rosy Crucifixion*?"

"No!"

"I'm going," I said. "I've screwed everything up."

"No, stay there, please!"

I noticed that he was reading with the same lightning-like rapidity with which I was accustomed to reading.

I looked up at the clock on the wall.

"I'm going. Thanks," I said, making my way toward the door.

"The fact is," he said, remaining seated and continuing to leaf through the pages, "that nothing is true in this manuscript. You have not liberated yourself from your personal history, you have invented another one by basing yourself on Jung."

"Yes! *Symbolik des Geistes*," I shouted back.

I rushed out, but he caught up with me.

"Look here, listen to me. Why don't you take a trip? Go to Paris, look up Guattari, Felix Guattari. Tell him that I've sent you . . . And write me, send me a couple letters, let me know . . . But go alone, leave the women be. Desire is limit, have you understood? Have you understood? Follow the Law."

Seated on the sidewalk of Park Avenue, almost next to the General Consulate of Italy, not far from Dr. Pépin's office, I wept out of rage.

4. Non, merci

Years back, as I noticed earlier, Ralph Pépin wanted to become a man.

"*Non, merci.*"

"*Tout reste inachevé. Il reste encore beacoup à dire.* Take the fever in your hands, lay it down on the snow. A flower will be born, you will not die."

Three or four of those tiny tin-plate planes passed overhead every day. They flew low, a gloved hand waved a greeting, and then they would disappear beyond the traps, toward the petrified lakes.

"Je t'aime sans raison, ma morte!"
"Non, merci."

5. The Letter

I think that I wrote him the longest letter of my life. I typed it. And I kept a copy of it.

> *My dear Ralph:*
>
> *I owe you a letter and I'm writing it from Sabbioneta, Italy, after a brief flight to Israel. I spent three days in Jaffa. I made love with the woman who was waiting for me in Rome from the United States. I saw three persons and flew back. I found myself alone in Milan. I wrote postcards to my wife, who lives now with a lover, and to an Indian girl who pilots small bush planes in Alaska. But in Mantua I met an old acquaintance. She was very young and so was I, but now she is married and saddled with children, unhappy and unfit. We banded together so as not to avoid the pangs of regrets after this new encounter. The real has become water.*

❑

What do you do, Ralph, when you meet the arcane and talk to it?

She had the face of infancy, of daisies in a meadow, of the kitchen range, of the educated shopper. She told me that she saw me studying lotus flowers on the banks of the Mincio, years and years ago. And it was true, because years and years ago I did study lotus flowers on the banks of the Mincio. She would watch me from a screened window. I answered, Yes. Years ago I studied the synthetic lotus at the suggestion of the Mantuan Piero Dallarana who, she told me, was her uncle. To which I replied that in that year, at least for me, Piero Dallarana was very much like Mantegna the painter.

There was a bar on the public square to which she led me. This woman of times past who nevertheless was dressed in the elegant Fiorucci fripperies. She told me sixteenth-century tales when the local lords kept a man, half-dead and half-alive, in a cage on the square, exhibited to the public. "Those were the cruel times of the Renaissance," she explained, "when a man, half-dead and half-alive, exhibited in a cage in the public square was a symbol of seigniorial power."

It was also the time in which her favorite artists signed contracts with the Tyrant. "But today the Tyrant is dead," I said, "and the Artist is still alive." But she, disinterestedly, observed that artists of that caliber no longer exist on earth, precisely because tyrants are dead. Artists today are quite ordinary people.

I replied that today tyrants have a different face and consequently the artists are also different. I told her about a town of a marine character, in Selimo, Italy, where love makes love with lilies of the valley, which have an abbey-like scent about them, and where funerals are still festive occasions, where the olive tree still sturdy.

I talked about my people and about their modesty, I talked about my people and about their pragmatism. I spoke with a nervous voice but my hands were motionless. I did not want to create a familiar stage setting.

How stupid, Death!

□

Now I typewrite what I've seen in the old city, in Tel Aviv, as I eat slices of eggplants fried in the holy oil.

Oak trunks, arranged in piles during the night, were burnt on the streets of the ghetto creating pillars of smoke. The black Jews who helped elect Begin now want to dump him. The apartments built for them cost more than they earn, so that they are occupied by those who have more money than one earns. Life costs so much here that one gets the impression that life counts for nothing.

There is nothing mystical about Israel. It's inhabited by a tough people, a people that has endured much, and that cannot forgive or forget. Yes. Never, never forget.

I see the collateral strata, the Arabs, camouflaged in the ghetto. It is a people that aspires to terrorism, to massacre. But they will change. They also yearn for peace.

My Jewish-American girlfriend, with whom I ate the eggplant slices in the Jaffa ghetto, watching the fires from the balcony, has decided to go to Jerusalem in order to enter a competition to which she will submit a proposal for the reconstruction of Noah's Ark.

It is to be set up in a zoo.

In fact, she invited me here to help her to sell the project. The special feature about the Ark would be its rebirth on the basis of its dimensions as described in Genesis.

❏

I flew back to take another look at Milan.

Love walks with me, but we never cut ourselves off from the ship-canal. We go into a bar, we come out of a bookstore, walk along the canal, and glance at the vanishing wine in the bottle. Boredom has the taste of silence and sultry bed sheets and when a spot, which is a drop of her sweat, falls on my hand, I cautiously gather it up with the thin blade of my fingernails and, out of modesty, I let it dry in the air.

I sleep without let-up and always dream. She never sleeps and torments me. She doesn't know me, we do not know each other, nevertheless she kisses my body as though it were water, and I kiss her back and her body feels like marble. She often drives away in her Alfa-Sud, staying away for hours at a time, but she always comes back with a different dress and with a bag of apples. She has a hamper-like purse in which she carries apples and she eats only these apples, even when we dine.

She often talks to me about her husband and her daughter, and of the two boys she has chosen to be her lovers.

The one she seduced, during a French lesson, is now eighteen but, at that time, he was fifteen. She went biking with her husband, and went to the movies with the boy. Eventually the husband found out, as did the boy's mother. Nothing really happened, save that the husband put all the property in his name, except for this villa which belongs to her. The boy now works as a mechanic in Mantua where her husband is the head physician in the hospital.

The other boy is twenty-three, very handsome, according to her. He is studying and living in Milan. But she truly loves the eighteen year old who, in turn, loves her ten-year-old daughter.

I find myself in the middle of this knotty situation, but it seems that she quintessentializes me in all her men, having found them again in one person. She, however, is the only one to perceive my mystery, which is that which always takes me away from emotions.

To her, love seems simple, but for me love is something that wears out. I tell her that love is something that is squandered, as we are doing now, and that love is that which is not, or that which will blossom soon. For love is never what you have: otherwise we would not be talking about it so much, as we are doing now, while walking along the canal in shorts. She says that she always makes love, and she likes to insult her partner and moan in order to get over the eternal threshold of the orgasm and achieve it in one final gasp. It's been a struggle that she has been waging for years, and she still doesn't know how much it might be worth.

With me there, no voice comes over the radio or from the television set, nor is there any J&B. When the play begins, always in the heat of the afternoon, it comes to a close only when the moon rises above the pine trees overlooking the canal.

It's always so simple, it's always without a word, but I always voyage through a whole life. And once again I see things that I had set aside: the nail clippers, for example, lost in India; the white dunes of thistle on Cape Cod over which I flew with a small plane; the impatient kiss I placed on the lips of the girl I loved after stopping the car at the roadside ditch in Georgia, as the result of which the car irretrievably sank in the thicket of the marshes, and we were set back on the road by a crane belonging to a group of K.K.K.

In my mind's eye I also recalled the tragic turn in Vermont, where a high tension wire split in two and fell in front of my speeding motorcycle, and I missed decapitation by a millimeter.

I see many things again, and it is always summer, even if certain things transpired in the snow.

Then she becomes increasingly more whorish and she wants my wrist watch, my ball pen, the address of a friend, a piece of my right calf which she tried to cut out with a razor blade. Finally she shaves off the hairs of that calf and makes a tiny pile of them on a sheet of cigarette paper which she folds and smokes, scorching the tip of her nose.

Now she has placed a Band-Aid on it and she has taken my socks and gone down to the canal to wash them, beating the wash on the stone of the graveled bank.

❑

I am reading *The Best of Sholem Aleichen* which I bought in Israel. And I come upon the pure Hebrew of the psalm, "Hamavdil beyn Koydesh l'khoyl," which means that some make chaff while others work.

I begin to pack my things; she's outside.

I walk on the bank of the canal but feel the presence of the dead or dying man in the cage of the Gonzagas. My invisible companion insists on taking my suitcase and I stubbornly refuse to give it to him. He's not breathing hard but he's walking fast, albeit in fits and starts without, however, passing me. He smokes and smokes and even takes a pill. At one time he was a pharmacist, but he never carried aspirin with him. He asks me if there's a relation between my trip to Nicaragua and my trip to Israel. I say no, I don't concern myself with politics. But he thinks I work, like Kafka, for a luminous and mysterious system. I reply brusquely that I tour here and there with the sole ambition of wanting to die.

Nano stops musing and finally he says: "You are an exceptional man, really. The more I look at you, the younger you seem."

"By necessity," I reply. "I was born in the time of Pliny. It's also as if the ashes had not touched me at all."

It is described by Umberto Eco in his translation of the letter of Pliny the Younger to Tacitus:

"He was in Misen where he commanded the fleet. Toward the seventh hour of August 24 my mother pointed out to him a cloud uncommon by its form and size. He had just been sunbathing, and then showered after which he stretched out to eat something and then to read. He asked for his sandals and went up to a site from which he could obtain a better view of that mysterious thing in the sky. A cloud was rising (and to anyone watching it, it was uncertain to determine the mountain of origin — only later did it become known that it was Vesuvius) and no other tree than a Mediterranean pine would have better suggested its form, with an extremely long trunk rising skyward and spreading in various branches everywhere. I believe it was being raised by a fresh wind and later, when the wind dropped, or when it was overcome by its own weight, it dissolved as it widened its spread, at times white, at times dirty and spotted, depending on whether it was carrying earth or ashes. The old man went to take a look, going as far as the shore where he fell asleep. This is how the ashes came to preserve him for us."

The man walking at my side finally admits to being tired and stretches himself out in a urn of water. He is thoroughly composed, the expression on his face is serious but not troubled and I look at him absentmindedly, as it were, because I am being drawn by the din of what sounds like a discotheque.

The sound turns out to be coming, instead, from the Town Hall. It rises on the canal where a festival with speeches is in progress. Three ladies are selling a box of curious items to arriving patrons, each one of which tells something about the man by whom it was crafted.

They flit about, taking and offering. They are wearing heavy cufflinks around their short necks, constantly and obsequiously followed by a tall man who looks like an athletic or a night bird type. They are chasing after a gentleman dressed in white who enters and exits from mysterious offices equipped with machines and microphones, wires and tapes. Finally they stop him in the middle of the wires, and the woman with the fish around her neck displays a pair of scissors, a well-known and advertised brand. The man dressed in white knows that she wants to cut his life, and he immobilizes her with the flash of his minuscule Argus which he always carries with him.

The man dressed in white is the inventor of the box, but the three women sell it as if it were their property.

When he's outside, the man finds himself on the bank of the canal again. Now two women are talking to him through the urn of water containing the dead man. Dressed like twins, they sport pinkish-colored hair and the custom jewelry they are wearing is as light as their young years. They are talking about that Mediterranean pine which is a cloud, at times white and at times spotted, depending on whether it is carrying earth or ashes.

There's the smell of water-lilies on the canal, soon the dawn of another life will break. I perceive the meaning of it and bid farewell to the companion who is lying still.

Pliny, too, had no inkling of his predestined misfortune.

6. *The Auction*

Ralph Pépin never replied or didn't know how to reply. Or his reply got lost forever, as often happens to certain things: friends, love, continents. Only solitude is inseparable.

A year ago, through the New York Times *Obituaries*, I learned of Ralph's death. He had died of AIDS. This is how I came to remember my book.

I went to New York. They told me that there would be an auction of the manuscripts, paintings, sculptures, cameos and other antiquarian items belonging to Dr. Pépin very soon, within a few days, in Montréal, his native city.

Everything had been sealed and assigned.

I had got in touch with the lawyer, a hirsute but cordial young man. He understood my predicament, yet he couldn't do anything. Besides, I had no documentation attesting ownership of "my" manuscript. True, they found the letter that I had sent from Italy. But even this was anonymous, that was not "mine." It was signed by "Anonimo Selimano." I showed the copy. Finally, it was the other, the hirsute young man, who said okay. Nevertheless I would have to go to Montréal to the auction so as not to muddle the legal proceedings further. The manuscript would be sold back to me and adjudicated for the symbolic sum of one dollar.

I flew back to Montréal.

There weren't many people, but persons and representatives of persons had come, so to speak, from all over: New York, Paris, Milan. Even from India. There were also publishers, literary agents, lawyers, and patients of Dr. Pépin. There was also his sister, Sylvie Pépin-Hull, a widow, with a house in Montréal (now rented) and another in New Wilmington, Pennsylvania.

"I never had any friendly relations with my brother. Throughout his life he remained a capricious baby, split in two," Sylvie Pépin-Hull confessed to me later in the hotel. And she added: "I was still a child when one day he took off for the Arctic just like that. He wanted to harden himself, learn from experience, he said. Instead he came back a frightened being. From that day on nobody recognized him anymore. He would have killed anyone."

"He was with me," I said. "I was also there."

7. *Accademia*

Ralph Pépin had read and annotated the manuscript. He had written his judgment, his opinion on each one. Some had been recommended for its publication. Mine, for example. And he suggested also the title: *Accademia*.

On it he had written a disclaimer as if to confirm that my work belonged to fantasy, not to the real:

> *The city in these pages is imaginary.*
> *The people, the places are all fictitious.*
> *Only the Academic routine is based on*
> *Established investigatory technique.*

"Beautiful!" I murmured to myself.

8. Autobiography

In the hotel I re-read the manuscript. I realized that it was a real novel in "autobiographical" form. I found myself outside it, as a writer, and inside it as a reader. I remembered some of those events vaguely; they were of a personal nature but the imaginary aspects — the language, for example — in effect had absorbed and distorted that which could be called reality.

Perhaps Ralph Pépin was right?

Impossible.

All I had done was to recount my personal history and that of another person dear to me, weaving a human and intellectual tapestry that I attributed to a husband, Simon, and to a wife, Lisa. Perhaps in order to distance myself from her? Perhaps to distance myself from myself?

What is autobiography?

Here are some opinions:

" . . . compared to tragedy, or epic, or lyric poetry, autobiography always looks slightly disreputable and self-indulgent in a way that may be symptomatic of its incompatibility with the monumental dignity of aesthetic values" (Paul de Man, "Autobiography as Defacement," *Modern Language Notes*, Vol. 95, No. 5, Dec. 1979, p. 919).

"Autobiography veils a defacement of the mind of which it is itself the cause" (*op. cit.*, p. 930).

"The autobiographer's impulse has synchronized with that of his fellow man; he is speaking not only to but for his contemporaries. That mood which engenders autobiography is known to many who do not take up the pen" (Elizabeth Bowen, "Autobiography as an Art" (*Saturday Review of Literature*, XXXIV, March 17, 1951, p. 10).

"If autobiographies could no longer rely upon the old spiritual verities and forms, they continued to pursue the blessed rage for order in their narratives" (Robert Bell: "Metamorphoses of Spiritual Autobiography," *ELG*, XLIV, 1977, p. 125).

" . . . Freud's and Jung's examples seem to put in question the conventional distinction between autobiography and fiction. When we look for other works embodying their understanding of how one tells one's story, we find ourselves looking primarily at writings we have been accustomed to read as novels. Proust's *Remembrance of Things Past,* Joyce's *Portrait* and *Ulysses . . . *" (Christine Downing, "Re-Visioning Autobiography: The Bequest of Freud and Jung," *Soundings*, LX, 1977, p. 227).

"The awareness of an aspect of myself radically other than my conscious ego implies also that autobiography emerges as the expression of a divided self. Id, ego, super-ego are Freud's terms; persona, ego, shadow, anima or animus are Jung's. Either way autobiography has become dramatic rather than lyric or epic: His Majesty the Ego can no longer assume that his voice will be the only one. Rousseau had already offered us a hero who could criticize his own heroic illusions, but now that heroic project too is undermined. Interpretation and Memories both reflect an acknowledgment of the fictiveness of the unity of the self" (*op. cit.*, p. 213).

"It is as literature, not as the private document, that modern autobiography makes its claim. It is the product not of licensed ease but of a disciplined concentration — in fact, no longer an amateur affair" (Elizabeth Bowen, *op. cit.*, p. 9).

Perhaps Ralph Pépin was right.

9. Misplacement

Sylvia Pépin-Hull had to sup. I, too.

This city's queer.

She was born and had lived here. I had been here so many times. I had resided here. I knew lots of people and neighborhoods and now it looked strange, foreign to her and to me alike.

This city's queer?

"Not at all," I said, walking toward a book shop on rue Sainte- Catherine. "We're the queer ones, because we live elsewhere. Are you a separatist?"

"*Je me souviens. Oui.* But I no longer have anyone here," she said. "I'm a migrant."

"I'm an exile."

"You're a migrant, too."

"I thought about it, many times. What is it?"

"To be misplaced."

"And how about in New Wilmington, Pennsylvania?"

"Hilly country, dry land, hoof beat echo on winding roads, corn and barns, a buggy, a hen, roast duck on Sunday, tapioca pudding, gasoline lamps. Simplicity, honesty, work. Hilly country, fence gates, cabbage slow, applesauce. They are Amish, simple, devout people. Nobody bothers me. I don't bother anybody. The days pass by, the nights too. It seem to me that I'm living in a white bed sheet.

"And your husband?"

"He died in a construction-site accident. He was an engineer, but he worked on the roofs. And one day an iron girder fell on him, and he flew down thirty storeys."

"Sorry!"

I found Jung, my book, in French. I leafed through it and read:

> *The animal, in its almost complete uncon-*
> *sciousness, was always the symbol of that psychic*
> *sphere of man that is hidden in the darkness of*
> *the corporeal instinct. The hero rides on the stal-*
> *lion, characterized by the equal feminine number*
> *4; the princess A. on the mare, that has only*
> *three legs (hence a male number). From these*
> *numbers it becomes evident that, with the trans-*
> *formation in animals, a certain change in the sex-*
> *ual character intervened: the stallion has a femi-*
> *nine attribute, the mare a masculine one.*

"I don't understand," she said.

"We are at the central point: *anima* and *animus*."

"I don't know. I don't know anything. What kind of a writer are you?"

"I just write," I said. And I took her by the arm. "I would like a good restaurant."

"And I a child . . . This wish comes to me from time to time, like now . . . But then it goes away. What are people to do with children? Do you have children?"

"Three," I said. And I looked at her, smiling.

We walked at a faster pace toward University Street and Rue McGill. In front of the restaurant a young man, attired à la Charlie Chaplin bowed, singing: *"Ma joie (ou mon douleur) chante le paysage."*

10. *Life with the Amish?*

Five days in that hotel. Sylvie Pépin-Hull read *Acca-demia*. She is a librarian. She never said anything about anything but understood that I've left open a possibility.

She was so diaphanous and whitish that I recalled: "It seems to me as though I live in a white bed sheet."

Then came the wind.

"Really?" she said.

"I'm on a sabbatical leave. I don't feel going abroad so soon, now."

"Why not my place?"

"Yeah! Why not your place?"

In my old debauchée's sport car we searched the map for the shortest route to New Wilmington, Pennsylvania, to start a new life among the Amish.

My god, the Amish?

About the Author

Giose Rimanelli was born in Italy on November 28, 1926, of an Italian father and a Canadian mother. He gained international fame with some of his novels during the 1950s, translated in many languages and also made into movies and radio plays, such as *The Day of the Lion* (1954), *Original Sin* (1957), *Third Class Ticket* (1958), *A Social Position* (1959). To his narrative activity he has added poetry, professional journalism, theater and literary criticism, both in Italian and in English. As for poetry, he has primarily engaged himself with Latin and Provençal poets whom he has translated, eventually leading him to the rediscovery of the dialect of his native Molise with the great songs and ballads of *Moliseide* (1990-1992) and *Musings* (1996).

He has lived for many years in both United States and Canada, teaching Italian and Comparative Literature in major universities. He was for a while (in 1953) chief editor of the Italian-Canadian weekly *Il cittadino canadese* of Montreal, and out of that experience he wrote the best-selling *Third Class Ticket* (1958). While teaching at the University of British Columbia (1963-65) he did research for the anthology *Modern Canadian Stories* (1967), which was adopted as a standard textbook in Canadian schools. He considers Canada his "subliminal" motherland. In 1977 he donated his correspondence and a bundle of his still unpublished manuscripts to the Fisher Rare Book Library of the University of Toronto, for future studies. In 1994, *Benedetta in Guysterland* won the American Book Award.

By the Same Author

Viamerica (1997)
From G. to G.: 101 Somnets (1996)
The Big Room (1996)
Detroit Blues (1996)
Musings (1996)
Dirige me Domine, Deus meus (1996)
Alien Cantica (1995)
Benedetta in Guysterland (1993)
Moliseide (1990, 1992)
Arcano (1990)
Time Hidden Between Lines (1986)
Molise Molise (1979)
Italian Literature: Roots and Branches (1978)
Graffiti (1977)
Poems Make Pictures Pictures Make Poems (1971)
Tragic America (1968)
Love Monks of the Middle Ages (1967)
Carmina blabla (1967)
Modern Canadian Stories (1966)
The Sneak Craft (1959)
A Social Position (1959)
Third Class Ticket (1958)
Original Sin (1957)
The Day of the Lion (1954)

The Guernica Prose Series

Eugene Mirabelli. *The World at Noon*. 1994

Madeleine Ouellette-Michalska. *The Sandwoman*. 1990

Ben Morreale. *The Loss of the Miraculous*. 1996

Miriam Packer. *Take Me to Coney Island*. 1993

Claude Péloquin. *A Dive into My Essence*. 1990

Pierre Yves Pépin. *American Stories*. 1996

Penny Petrone. *Breaking the Mould*. 1995

Giose Rimanelli. *Accademia.*1997

Giose Rimanelli. *Benedetta in Guysterland*. 1993 (American Book Award 1994)

Francis Simard. *Talking It Out: The October Crisis from the Inside*. 1987

Stendhal. *The Life of Mozart*. 1991

France Théoret. *The Tangible Word*. 1991

Anthony Valerio. *Conversation with Johnny*. 1997

Anthony Valerio. *The Mediterranean Runs Through Brooklyn*. 1997

Anthony Valerio. *Valentino and the Great Italians*. 1994

Yolande Villemaire. *Amazon Angel*. 1993

Robert Viscusi. *Astoria*. 1994 (American Book Award 1996)

AGMV
MARQUIS
Québec, Canada
1997